The Way of the World

A COMEDY

William Congreve

HAWK PRESS

Published by

Hawk Press
4836/24, Ansari Road, Daryaganj
New Delhi – 110 002
Phones : 9643330713, +91-11-23278618, +91-11-35676207
E-mail : thehawkpress@gmail.com
www.thehawkpress.com

ISBN : 978-93-93971-41-8

To the Right Honourable
Ralph, Earl of Mountague, Etc.

My Lord,—Whether the world will arraign me of vanity or not, that I have presumed to dedicate this comedy to your lordship, I am yet in doubt; though, it may be, it is some degree of vanity even to doubt of it. One who has at any time had the honour of your lordship's conversation, cannot be supposed to think very meanly of that which he would prefer to your perusal. Yet it were to incur the imputation of too much sufficiency to pretend to such a merit as might abide the test of your lordship's censure.

Whatever value may be wanting to this play while yet it is mine, will be sufficiently made up to it when it is once become your lordship's; and it is my security, that I cannot have overrated it more by my dedication than your lordship will dignify it by your patronage.

That it succeeded on the stage was almost beyond my expectation; for but little of it was prepared for that general taste which seems now to be predominant in the palates of our audience.

Those characters which are meant to be ridiculed in most of our comedies are of fools so gross, that in my humble opinion they should rather disturb than divert the well-natured and reflecting part of an audience; they are rather objects of charity than contempt, and instead of moving our mirth, they ought very often to excite our compassion.

This reflection moved me to design some characters which should appear ridiculous not so much through a natural folly (which is incorrigible, and therefore not proper for the stage) as through an affected wit: a wit which, at the same time that it is affected, is also false. As there is some difficulty in the formation of a character of this nature, so there is some hazard which attends the progress of its success upon the stage: for many come to a play so overcharged with criticism, that they very often let fly their censure, when through their rashness they have mistaken their aim. This I had occasion lately to observe: for this play had been acted two or three days before some of these hasty judges could find the leisure to distinguish betwixt the character of a Witwoud and a Truewit.

I must beg your lordship's pardon for this digression from the true course of this epistle; but that it may not seem altogether impertinent, I beg that I may plead the occasion of it, in part of that excuse of which I stand in need, for recommending this comedy to your protection. It is only by the countenance of your lordship, and the few so qualified, that such who write with care and pains can hope to be distinguished: for the prostituted name of poet promiscuously levels all that bear it.

Terence, the most correct writer in the world, had a Scipio and a Lelius, if not to assist him, at least to support him in his reputation. And notwithstanding his extraordinary merit, it may be their countenance was not more than necessary.

The purity of his style, the delicacy of his turns, and the justness of his characters, were all of them beauties which the greater part of his audience were incapable of tasting. Some of the coarsest strokes of Plautus, so severely censured by Horace, were more likely to affect the multitude; such, who come with expectation to laugh at the last act of a play, and are better entertained with two or three unseasonable jests than with the artful solution of the fable.

As Terence excelled in his performances, so had he great advantages to encourage his undertakings, for he built most on the foundations of Menander: his plots were generally modelled, and his characters ready drawn to his hand. He copied Menander; and Menander had no less light in the formation of his characters from the observations of Theophrastus, of whom he was a disciple; and Theophrastus, it is known, was not only the disciple, but the immediate successor of Aristotle, the first and greatest judge of poetry. These were great models to design by; and the further advantage which Terence possessed towards giving his plays the due ornaments of purity of style, and justness of manners, was not less considerable from the freedom of conversation which was permitted him with Lelius and Scipio, two of the greatest and most polite men of his age. And, indeed, the privilege of such a conversation is the only certain means of attaining to the perfection of dialogue.

If it has happened in any part of this comedy that I have gained a turn of style or expression more correct, or at least more corrigible, than in those which I have formerly written, I must, with equal pride and gratitude, ascribe it to the honour of your lordship's admitting me into your conversation, and that of a society where everybody else was so well worthy of you, in your retirement last summer from the town: for it was immediately after, that this comedy was written. If I have failed in my performance, it is only to be regretted, where there were so many not inferior either to a Scipio or a Lelius, that there should be one wanting equal in capacity to a Terence.

If I am not mistaken, poetry is almost the only art which has not yet laid claim to your lordship's patronage. Architecture and painting, to the great honour of our country, have flourished under your influence and protection. In the meantime, poetry, the eldest sister of all arts, and parent of most, seems to have resigned her birthright, by having neglected to pay her duty to your lordship, and by permitting others of a later extraction to prepossess that place in your esteem, to which none can pretend a better title. Poetry, in its nature, is sacred to the good and great: the relation between them is reciprocal, and they are ever propitious to it. It is the privilege of poetry to address them, and it is their prerogative alone to give it protection.

This received maxim is a general apology for all writers who consecrate their labours to great men: but I could wish, at this time, that this address were exempted from the common pretence of all dedications; and that as I can distinguish your lordship even among the most deserving, so this offering might become remarkable by some particular instance of respect, which should assure your lordship that I am, with all due sense of your extreme worthiness and humanity, my lord, your lordship's most obedient and most obliged humble servant,

WILL. CONGREVE.

PROLOGUE.

Spoken by Mr. Betterton.

Of those few fools, who with ill stars are curst,
Sure scribbling fools, called poets, fare the worst:
For they're a sort of fools which fortune makes,
And, after she has made 'em fools, forsakes.
With Nature's oafs 'tis quite a diff'rent case,
For Fortune favours all her idiot race.
In her own nest the cuckoo eggs we find,
O'er which she broods to hatch the changeling kind:
No portion for her own she has to spare,
So much she dotes on her adopted care.

Poets are bubbles, by the town drawn in,
Suffered at first some trifling stakes to win:
But what unequal hazards do they run!
Each time they write they venture all they've won:
The Squire that's buttered still, is sure to be undone.
This author, heretofore, has found your favour,
But pleads no merit from his past behaviour.
To build on that might prove a vain presumption,
Should grants to poets made admit resumption,
And in Parnassus he must lose his seat,
If that be found a forfeited estate.

He owns, with toil he wrought the following scenes,
But if they're naught ne'er spare him for his pains:

Damn him the more; have no commiseration
For dulness on mature deliberation.
He swears he'll not resent one hissed-off scene,
Nor, like those peevish wits, his play maintain,
Who, to assert their sense, your taste arraign.
Some plot we think he has, and some new thought;
Some humour too, no farce—but that's a fault.
Satire, he thinks, you ought not to expect;
For so reformed a town who dares correct?
To please, this time, has been his sole pretence,
He'll not instruct, lest it should give offence.
Should he by chance a knave or fool expose,
That hurts none here, sure here are none of those.
In short, our play shall (with your leave to show it)
Give you one instance of a passive poet,
Who to your judgments yields all resignation:
So save or damn, after your own discretion.

DRAMATIS PERSONÆ.

MEN.	
Fainall, in love with Mrs. Marwood,	Mr. Betterton.
Mirabell, in love with Mrs. Millamant,	Mr. Verbruggen.
Witwoud, follower of Mrs. Millamant,	Mr. Bowen.
Petulant, follower of Mrs. Millamant,	Mr. Bowman.
Sir Wilfull Witwoud, half brother to Witwoud, and nephew to Lady Wishfort,	Mr. Underhill.
Waitwell, servant to Mirabell,	Mr. Bright.
WOMEN.	
Lady Wishfort, enemy to Mirabell, for having falsely pretended love to her,	Mrs. Leigh.
Mrs. Millamant, a fine lady, niece to Lady Wishfort, and loves Mirabell,	Mrs. Bracegirdle.
Mrs. Marwood, friend to Mr. Fainall, and likes Mirabell,	Mrs. Barry.
Mrs. Fainall, daughter to Lady Wishfort, and wife to Fainall, formerly friend to Mirabell,	Mrs. Bowman.
Foible, woman to Lady Wishfort,	Mrs. Willis.
Mincing, woman to Mrs. Millamant,	Mrs. Prince.

Dancers, Footmen, Attendants.

Scene: London.

The time equal to that of the presentation.

ACT I.—SCENE I.

A Chocolate-house.

Mirabell and Fainall rising from cards. Betty waiting.

MIRA. You are a fortunate man, Mr. Fainall.

FAIN. Have we done?

MIRA. What you please. I'll play on to entertain you.

FAIN. No, I'll give you your revenge another time, when you are not so indifferent; you are thinking of something else now, and play too negligently: the coldness of a losing gamester lessens the pleasure of the winner. I'd no more play with a man that slighted his ill fortune than I'd make love to a woman who undervalued the loss of her reputation.

MIRA. You have a taste extremely delicate, and are for refining on your pleasures.

FAIN. Prithee, why so reserved? Something has put you out of humour.

MIRA. Not at all: I happen to be grave to-day, and you are gay; that's all.

FAIN. Confess, Millamant and you quarrelled last night, after I left you; my fair cousin has some humours that would tempt the patience of a Stoic. What, some coxcomb came in, and was well received by her, while you were by?

MIRA. Witwoud and Petulant, and what was worse, her aunt, your wife's mother, my evil genius—or to sum up all in her own name, my old Lady Wishfort came in.

FAIN. Oh, there it is then: she has a lasting passion for you, and with reason.—What, then my wife was there?

MIRA. Yes, and Mrs. Marwood and three or four more, whom I never saw before; seeing me, they all put on their grave faces, whispered one another, then complained aloud of the vapours, and after fell into a profound silence.

FAIN. They had a mind to be rid of you.

MIRA. For which reason I resolved not to stir. At last the good old lady broke through her painful taciturnity with an invective against long visits. I would not have understood her, but Millamant joining in the argument, I rose and with a constrained smile told her, I thought nothing was so easy as to know when a visit began to be troublesome; she reddened and I withdrew, without expecting her reply.

FAIN. You were to blame to resent what she spoke only in compliance with her aunt.

MIRA. She is more mistress of herself than to be under the necessity of such a resignation.

FAIN. What? though half her fortune depends upon her marrying with my lady's approbation?

MIRA. I was then in such a humour, that I should have been better pleased if she had been less discreet.

FAIN. Now I remember, I wonder not they were weary of you; last night was one of their cabal-nights: they have 'em three times a week and meet by turns at one another's apartments, where they come together like the coroner's inquest, to sit upon the murdered reputations of the week. You and I are excluded, and it was once proposed that all the male sex should be excepted; but somebody moved that to avoid scandal there might be one man of the community, upon which motion Witwoud and Petulant were enrolled members.

MIRA. And who may have been the foundress of this sect? My Lady Wishfort, I warrant, who publishes her detestation of mankind, and full of the vigour of fifty-five, declares for a friend and ratafia; and let posterity shift for itself, she'll breed no more.

FAIN. The discovery of your sham addresses to her, to conceal your love to her niece, has provoked this separation. Had you dissembled better, things might have continued in the state of nature.

MIRA. I did as much as man could, with any reasonable conscience; I proceeded to the very last act of flattery with her, and was guilty of a song in her commendation. Nay, I got a friend to put her into a lampoon, and compliment her with the imputation of an affair with a young fellow, which I carried so far, that I told her the malicious town took notice that she was grown fat of a sudden; and when she lay in of a dropsy, persuaded her she was reported to be in labour. The devil's in't, if an old woman is to be flattered further, unless a man should endeavour downright personally to debauch her: and that my virtue forbade me. But for the discovery of this amour, I am indebted to your friend, or your wife's friend, Mrs. Marwood.

FAIN. What should provoke her to be your enemy, unless she has made you advances which you have slighted? Women do not easily forgive omissions of that nature.

MIRA. She was always civil to me, till of late. I confess I am not one of those coxcombs who are apt to interpret a woman's good manners to her prejudice, and think that she who does not refuse 'em everything can refuse 'em nothing.

FAIN. You are a gallant man, Mirabell; and though you may have cruelty enough not to satisfy a lady's longing, you have too much generosity not to be tender of her honour. Yet you speak with an indifference which seems to be affected, and confesses you are conscious of a negligence.

MIRA. You pursue the argument with a distrust that seems to be unaffected, and confesses you are conscious of a concern for which the lady is more indebted to you than is your wife.

FAIN. Fie, fie, friend, if you grow censorious I must leave you:—I'll look upon the gamesters in the next room.

MIRA. Who are they?

FAIN. Petulant and Witwoud.—Bring me some chocolate.

MIRA. Betty, what says your clock?

BET. Turned of the last canonical hour, sir.

MIRA. How pertinently the jade answers me! Ha! almost one a' clock! [Looking on his watch.] Oh, y'are come!

SCENE II.

Mirabell and Footman.

MIRA. Well, is the grand affair over? You have been something tedious.

SERV. Sir, there's such coupling at Pancras that they stand behind one another, as 'twere in a country-dance. Ours was the last couple to lead up; and no hopes appearing of dispatch, besides, the parson growing hoarse, we were afraid his lungs would have failed before it came to our turn; so we drove round to Duke's Place, and there they were riveted in a trice.

MIRA. So, so; you are sure they are married?

SERV. Married and bedded, sir; I am witness.

MIRA. Have you the certificate?

SERV. Here it is, sir.

MIRA. Has the tailor brought Waitwell's clothes home, and the new liveries?

SERV. Yes, sir.

MIRA. That's well. Do you go home again, d'ye hear, and adjourn the consummation till farther order; bid Waitwell shake his ears, and Dame Partlet rustle up her feathers, and meet me at one a' clock by Rosamond's pond, that I may see her before she returns to her lady. And, as you tender your ears, be secret.

SCENE III.

Mirabell, Fainall, Betty.

FAIN. Joy of your success, Mirabell; you look pleased.

MIRA. Ay; I have been engaged in a matter of some sort of mirth, which is not yet ripe for discovery. I am glad this is not a cabal-night. I wonder, Fainall, that you who are married, and of consequence should be discreet, will suffer your wife to be of such a party.

FAIN. Faith, I am not jealous. Besides, most who are engaged are women and relations; and for the men, they are of a kind too contemptible to give scandal.

MIRA. I am of another opinion: the greater the coxcomb, always the more the scandal; for a woman who is not a fool can have but one reason for associating with a man who is one.

FAIN. Are you jealous as often as you see Witwoud entertained by Millamant?

MIRA. Of her understanding I am, if not of her person.

FAIN. You do her wrong; for, to give her her due, she has wit.

MIRA. She has beauty enough to make any man think so, and complaisance enough not to contradict him who shall tell her so.

FAIN. For a passionate lover methinks you are a man somewhat too discerning in the failings of your mistress.

MIRA. And for a discerning man somewhat too passionate a lover, for I like her with all her faults; nay, like her for her faults. Her follies are so natural, or so artful, that they become her, and those affectations which in another woman would be odious serve but to make her more agreeable. I'll tell thee, Fainall, she once used me with that insolence that in revenge I took her to pieces, sifted her, and separated her failings: I studied 'em and got 'em by rote. The catalogue was so large that I was not without hopes, one day or other, to hate her heartily. To which end I so used myself to think of 'em, that at length, contrary to my design and expectation, they gave me every hour less and less disturbance, till in a few days it became habitual to me to remember 'em without being displeased. They are now grown as familiar to me as my own frailties, and in all probability in a little time longer I shall like 'em as well.

FAIN. Marry her, marry her; be half as well acquainted with her charms as you are with her defects, and, my life on't, you are your own man again.

MIRA. Say you so?

FAIN. Ay, ay; I have experience. I have a wife, and so forth.

SCENE IV.

[To them] Messenger.

MESS. Is one Squire Witwoud here?

BET. Yes; what's your business?

MESS. I have a letter for him, from his brother Sir Wilfull, which I am charged to deliver into his own hands.

BET. He's in the next room, friend. That way.

SCENE V.

Mirabell, Fainall, Betty.

MIRA. What, is the chief of that noble family in town, Sir Wilfull Witwoud?

FAIN. He is expected to-day. Do you know him?

MIRA. I have seen him; he promises to be an extraordinary person. I think you have the honour to be related to him.

FAIN. Yes; he is half-brother to this Witwoud by a former wife, who was sister to my Lady Wishfort, my wife's mother. If you marry Millamant, you must call cousins too.

MIRA. I had rather be his relation than his acquaintance.

FAIN. He comes to town in order to equip himself for travel.

MIRA. For travel! Why the man that I mean is above forty.

FAIN. No matter for that; 'tis for the honour of England that all Europe should know we have blockheads of all ages.

MIRA. I wonder there is not an act of parliament to save the credit of the nation and prohibit the exportation of fools.

FAIN. By no means, 'tis better as 'tis; 'tis better to trade with a little loss, than to be quite eaten up with being overstocked.

MIRA. Pray, are the follies of this knight-errant and those of the squire, his brother, anything related?

FAIN. Not at all: Witwoud grows by the knight like a medlar grafted on a crab. One will melt in your mouth and t'other set your teeth on edge; one is all pulp and the other all core.

MIRA. So one will be rotten before he be ripe, and the other will be rotten without ever being ripe at all.

FAIN. Sir Wilfull is an odd mixture of bashfulness and obstinacy. But when he's drunk, he's as loving as the monster in The Tempest, and much after the same manner. To give bother his due, he has something of good-nature, and does not always want wit.

MIRA. Not always: but as often as his memory fails him and his commonplace of comparisons. He is a fool with a good memory and some few scraps of other folks' wit. He is one whose conversation can never be approved, yet it is now and then to be endured. He has indeed one good quality: he is not exceptious, for he so passionately affects the reputation of understanding raillery that he will construe an affront into a jest, and call downright rudeness and ill language satire and fire.

FAIN. If you have a mind to finish his picture, you have an opportunity to do it at full length. Behold the original.

SCENE VI.

[To them] Witwoud.

WIT. Afford me your compassion, my dears; pity me, Fainall, Mirabell, pity me.

MIRA. I do from my soul.

FAIN. Why, what's the matter?

WIT. No letters for me, Betty?

BET. Did not a messenger bring you one but now, sir?

WIT. Ay; but no other?

BET. No, sir.

WIT. That's hard, that's very hard. A messenger, a mule, a beast of burden, he has brought me a letter from the fool my brother, as heavy as a panegyric in a funeral sermon, or a copy of commendatory verses from one poet to another. And what's worse, 'tis as sure a forerunner of the author as an epistle dedicatory.

MIRA. A fool, and your brother, Witwoud?

WIT. Ay, ay, my half-brother. My half-brother he is, no nearer, upon honour.

MIRA. Then 'tis possible he may be but half a fool.

WIT. Good, good, Mirabell, le drôle! Good, good, hang him, don't let's talk of him.—Fainall, how does your lady? Gad, I say anything in the world to get this fellow out of my head. I beg pardon that I should ask a man of pleasure and the town a question at once so foreign and domestic. But I talk like an old maid at a marriage, I don't know what I say: but she's the best woman in the world.

FAIN. 'Tis well you don't know what you say, or else your commendation would go near to make me either vain or jealous.

WIT. No man in town lives well with a wife but Fainall. Your judgment, Mirabell?

MIRA. You had better step and ask his wife, if you would be credibly informed.

WIT. Mirabell!

MIRA. Ay.

WIT. My dear, I ask ten thousand pardons. Gad, I have forgot what I was going to say to you.

MIRA. I thank you heartily, heartily.

WIT. No, but prithee excuse me:—my memory is such a memory.

MIRA. Have a care of such apologies, Witwoud; for I never knew a fool but he affected to complain either of the spleen or his memory.

FAIN. What have you done with Petulant?

WIT. He's reckoning his money; my money it was: I have no luck to-day.

FAIN. You may allow him to win of you at play, for you are sure to be too hard for him at repartee: since you monopolise the wit that is between you, the fortune must be his of course.

MIRA. I don't find that Petulant confesses the superiority of wit to be your talent, Witwoud.

WIT. Come, come, you are malicious now, and would breed debates. Petulant's my friend, and a very honest fellow, and a very pretty fellow, and has a smattering—faith and troth, a pretty deal of an odd sort of a small wit: nay, I'll do him justice. I'm his friend, I won't wrong him. And if he had any judgment in the world, he would not be altogether contemptible. Come, come, don't detract from the merits of my friend.

FAIN. You don't take your friend to be over-nicely bred?

WIT. No, no, hang him, the rogue has no manners at all, that I must own; no more breeding than a bum-baily, that I grant you:—'tis pity; the fellow has fire and life.

MIRA. What, courage?

WIT. Hum, faith, I don't know as to that, I can't say as to that. Yes, faith, in a controversy he'll contradict anybody.

MIRA. Though 'twere a man whom he feared or a woman whom he loved.

WIT. Well, well, he does not always think before he speaks. We have all our failings; you are too hard upon him, you are, faith. Let me excuse him,—I can defend most of his faults, except one or two; one he has, that's the truth on't,—if he were my brother I could not acquit him—that indeed I could wish were otherwise.

MIRA. Ay, marry, what's that, Witwoud?

WIT. Oh, pardon me. Expose the infirmities of my friend? No, my dear, excuse me there.

FAIN. What, I warrant he's unsincere, or 'tis some such trifle.

WIT. No, no; what if he be? 'Tis no matter for that, his wit will excuse that. A wit should no more be sincere than a woman constant: one argues a decay of parts, as t'other of beauty.

MIRA. Maybe you think him too positive?

WIT. No, no; his being positive is an incentive to argument, and keeps up conversation.

FAIN. Too illiterate?

WIT. That? That's his happiness. His want of learning gives him the more opportunities to show his natural parts.

MIRA. He wants words?

WIT. Ay; but I like him for that now: for his want of words gives me the pleasure very often to explain his meaning.

FAIN. He's impudent?

WIT. No that's not it.

MIRA. Vain?

WIT. No.

MIRA. What, he speaks unseasonable truths sometimes, because he has not wit enough to invent an evasion?

WIT. Truths? Ha, ha, ha! No, no, since you will have it, I mean he never speaks truth at all, that's all. He will lie like a chambermaid, or a woman of quality's porter. Now that is a fault.

SCENE VII.

[To them] Coachman.

COACH. Is Master Petulant here, mistress?

BET. Yes.

COACH. Three gentlewomen in a coach would speak with him.

FAIN. O brave Petulant! Three!

BET. I'll tell him.

COACH. You must bring two dishes of chocolate and a glass of cinnamon water.

SCENE VIII.

Mirabell, Fainall, Witwoud.

WIT. That should be for two fasting strumpets, and a bawd troubled with wind. Now you may know what the three are.

MIRA. You are very free with your friend's acquaintance.

WIT. Ay, ay; friendship without freedom is as dull as love without enjoyment or wine without toasting: but to tell you a secret, these are trulls whom he allows coach-hire, and something more by the week, to call on him once a day at public places.

MIRA. How!

WIT. You shall see he won't go to 'em because there's no more company here to take notice of him. Why, this is nothing to what he used to do:—before he found out this way, I have known him call for himself—

FAIN. Call for himself? What dost thou mean?

WIT. Mean? Why he would slip you out of this chocolate-house, just when you had been talking to him. As soon as your back was turned—whip he was gone; then trip to his lodging, clap on a hood and scarf and a mask, slap into a hackney-coach, and drive hither to the door again in a trice; where he would send in for himself; that I mean, call for himself, wait for himself, nay, and what's more, not finding himself, sometimes leave a letter for himself.

MIRA. I confess this is something extraordinary. I believe he waits for himself now, he is so long a coming; oh, I ask his pardon.

SCENE IX.

Petulant, Mirabell, Fainall, Witwoud, Betty.

BET. Sir, the coach stays.

PET. Well, well, I come. 'Sbud, a man had as good be a professed midwife as a professed whoremaster, at this rate; to be knocked up and raised at all hours, and in all places. Pox on 'em, I won't come. D'ye hear, tell 'em I won't come. Let 'em snivel and cry their hearts out.

FAIN. You are very cruel, Petulant.

PET. All's one, let it pass. I have a humour to be cruel.

MIRA. I hope they are not persons of condition that you use at this rate.

PET. Condition? Condition's a dried fig, if I am not in humour. By this hand, if they were your—a—a—your what-d'ee-call-'ems themselves, they must wait or rub off, if I want appetite.

MIRA. What-d'ee-call-'ems! What are they, Witwoud?

WIT. Empresses, my dear. By your what-d'ee-call-'ems he means Sultana Queens.

PET. Ay, Roxolanas.

MIRA. Cry you mercy.

FAIN. Witwoud says they are—

PET. What does he say th'are?

WIT. I? Fine ladies, I say.

PET. Pass on, Witwoud. Harkee, by this light, his relations—two co-heiresses his cousins, and an old aunt, who loves cater-wauling better than a conventicle.

WIT. Ha, ha, ha! I had a mind to see how the rogue would come off. Ha, ha, ha! Gad, I can't be angry with him, if he had said they were my mother and my sisters.

MIRA. No?

WIT. No; the rogue's wit and readiness of invention charm me, dear Petulant.

BET. They are gone, sir, in great anger.

PET. Enough, let 'em trundle. Anger helps complexion, saves paint.

FAIN. This continence is all dissembled; this is in order to have something to brag of the next time he makes court to Millamant, and swear he has abandoned the whole sex for her sake.

MIRA. Have you not left off your impudent pretensions there yet? I shall cut your throat, sometime or other, Petulant, about that business.

PET. Ay, ay, let that pass. There are other throats to be cut.

MIRA. Meaning mine, sir?

PET. Not I—I mean nobody—I know nothing. But there are uncles and nephews in the world—and they may be rivals. What then? All's one for that.

MIRA. How? Harkee, Petulant, come hither. Explain, or I shall call your interpreter.

PET. Explain? I know nothing. Why, you have an uncle, have you not, lately come to town, and lodges by my Lady Wishfort's?

MIRA. True.

PET. Why, that's enough. You and he are not friends; and if he should marry and have a child, yon may be disinherited, ha!

MIRA. Where hast thou stumbled upon all this truth?

PET. All's one for that; why, then, say I know something.

MIRA. Come, thou art an honest fellow, Petulant, and shalt make love to my mistress, thou shalt, faith. What hast thou heard of my uncle?

PET. I? Nothing, I. If throats are to be cut, let swords clash. Snug's the word; I shrug and am silent.

MIRA. Oh, raillery, raillery! Come, I know thou art in the women's secrets. What, you're a cabalist; I know you stayed at Millamant's last night after I went. Was there any mention made of my uncle or me? Tell me; if thou hadst but good nature equal to thy wit, Petulant, Tony Witwoud, who is now thy competitor in fame, would show as dim by thee as a dead whiting's eye by a pearl of orient; he would no more be seen by thee than Mercury is by the sun: come, I'm sure thou wo't tell me.

PET. If I do, will you grant me common sense, then, for the future?

MIRA. Faith, I'll do what I can for thee, and I'll pray that heav'n may grant it thee in the meantime.

PET. Well, harkee.

FAIN. Petulant and you both will find Mirabell as warm a rival as a lover.

WIT. Pshaw, pshaw, that she laughs at Petulant is plain. And for my part, but that it is almost a fashion to admire her, I should—harkee—to tell you a secret, but let it go no further between friends, I shall never break my heart for her.

FAIN. How?

WIT. She's handsome; but she's a sort of an uncertain woman.

FAIN. I thought you had died for her.

WIT. Umh—no—

FAIN. She has wit.

WIT. 'Tis what she will hardly allow anybody else. Now, demme, I should hate that, if she were as handsome as Cleopatra. Mirabell is not so sure of her as he thinks for.

FAIN. Why do you think so?

WIT. We stayed pretty late there last night, and heard something of an uncle to Mirabell, who is lately come to town, and is between him and the best part of his estate. Mirabell and he are at some distance, as my Lady Wishfort has been told; and you know she hates Mirabell worse than a quaker hates a parrot, or than a fishmonger hates a hard frost. Whether this uncle has seen Mrs. Millamant or not, I cannot say; but there were items of such a treaty being in embryo; and if it should come to life, poor Mirabell would be in some sort unfortunately fobbed, i'faith.

FAIN. 'Tis impossible Millamant should hearken to it.

WIT. Faith, my dear, I can't tell; she's a woman and a kind of a humorist.

MIRA. And this is the sum of what you could collect last night?

PET. The quintessence. Maybe Witwoud knows more; he stayed longer. Besides, they never mind him; they say anything before him.

MIRA. I thought you had been the greatest favourite.

PET. Ay, tête-à-tête; but not in public, because I make remarks.

MIRA. You do?

PET. Ay, ay, pox, I'm malicious, man. Now he's soft, you know, they are not in awe of him. The fellow's well bred, he's what you call a—what d'ye-call-'em—a fine gentleman, but he's silly withal.

MIRA. I thank you, I know as much as my curiosity requires. Fainall, are you for the Mall?

FAIN. Ay, I'll take a turn before dinner.

WIT. Ay, we'll all walk in the park; the ladies talked of being there.

MIRA. I thought you were obliged to watch for your brother Sir Wilfull's arrival.

WIT. No, no, he comes to his aunt's, my Lady Wishfort; pox on him, I shall be troubled with him too; what shall I do with the fool?

PET. Beg him for his estate, that I may beg you afterwards, and so have but one trouble with you both.

WIT. O rare Petulant, thou art as quick as fire in a frosty morning; thou shalt to the Mall with us, and we'll be very severe.

PET. Enough; I'm in a humour to be severe.

MIRA. Are you? Pray then walk by yourselves. Let not us be accessory to your putting the ladies out of countenance with your senseless ribaldry, which you roar out aloud as often as they pass by you, and when you have made a handsome woman blush, then you think you have been severe.

PET. What, what? Then let 'em either show their innocence by not understanding what they hear, or else show their discretion by not hearing what they would not be thought to understand.

MIRA. But hast not thou then sense enough to know that thou ought'st to be most ashamed thyself when thou hast put another out of countenance?

PET. Not I, by this hand: I always take blushing either for a sign of guilt or ill-breeding.

MIRA. I confess you ought to think so. You are in the right, that you may plead the error of your judgment in defence of your practice.

Where modesty's ill manners, 'tis but fit

That impudence and malice pass for wit.

ACT II.—SCENE I.

St. James's Park.

Mrs. Fainall and Mrs. Marwood.

MRS. FAIN. Ay, ay, dear Marwood, if we will be happy, we must find the means in ourselves, and among ourselves. Men are ever in extremes; either doting or averse. While they are lovers, if they have fire and sense, their jealousies are insupportable: and when they cease to love (we ought to think at least) they loathe, they look upon us with horror and distaste, they meet us like the ghosts of what we were, and as from such, fly from us.

MRS. MAR. True, 'tis an unhappy circumstance of life that love should ever die before us, and that the man so often should outlive the lover. But say what you will, 'tis better to be left than never to have been loved. To pass our youth in dull indifference, to refuse the sweets of life because they once must leave us, is as preposterous as to wish to have been born old, because we one day must be old. For my part, my youth may wear and waste, but it shall never rust in my possession.

MRS. FAIN. Then it seems you dissemble an aversion to mankind only in compliance to my mother's humour.

MRS. MAR. Certainly. To be free, I have no taste of those insipid dry discourses with which our sex of force must entertain themselves apart from men. We may affect endearments to each other, profess eternal friendships, and seem to dote like lovers; but 'tis not in our natures long to persevere. Love will resume his empire in our breasts, and every heart, or soon or late, receive and readmit him as its lawful tyrant.

MRS. FAIN. Bless me, how have I been deceived! Why, you profess a libertine.

MRS. MAR. You see my friendship by my freedom. Come, be as sincere, acknowledge that your sentiments agree with mine.

MRS. FAIN. Never.

MRS. MAR. You hate mankind?

MRS. FAIN. Heartily, inveterately.

MRS. MAR. Your husband?

MRS. FAIN. Most transcendently; ay, though I say it, meritoriously.

MRS. MAR. Give me your hand upon it.

MRS. FAIN. There.

MRS. MAR. I join with you; what I have said has been to try you.

MRS. FAIN. Is it possible? Dost thou hate those vipers, men?

MRS. MAR. I have done hating 'em, and am now come to despise 'em; the next thing I have to do is eternally to forget 'em.

MRS. FAIN. There spoke the spirit of an Amazon, a Penthesilea.

MRS. MAR. And yet I am thinking sometimes to carry my aversion further.

MRS. FAIN. How?

MRS. MAR. Faith, by marrying; if I could but find one that loved me very well, and would be throughly sensible of ill usage, I think I should do myself the violence of undergoing the ceremony.

MRS. FAIN. You would not make him a cuckold?

MRS. MAR. No; but I'd make him believe I did, and that's as bad.

MRS. FAIN. Why had not you as good do it?

MRS. MAR. Oh, if he should ever discover it, he would then know the worst, and be out of his pain; but I would have him ever to continue upon the rack of fear and jealousy.

MRS. FAIN. Ingenious mischief! Would thou wert married to Mirabell.

MRS. MAR. Would I were.

MRS. FAIN. You change colour.

MRS. MAR. Because I hate him.

MRS. FAIN. So do I; but I can hear him named. But what reason have you to hate him in particular?

MRS. MAR. I never loved him; he is, and always was, insufferably proud.

MRS. FAIN. By the reason you give for your aversion, one would think it dissembled; for you have laid a fault to his charge, of which his enemies must acquit him.

MRS. MAR. Oh, then it seems you are one of his favourable enemies. Methinks you look a little pale, and now you flush again.

MRS. FAIN. Do I? I think I am a little sick o' the sudden.

MRS. MAR. What ails you?

MRS. FAIN. My husband. Don't you see him? He turned short upon me unawares, and has almost overcome me.

SCENE II.

[To them] Fainall and Mirabell.

MRS. MAR. Ha, ha, ha! he comes opportunely for you.

MRS. FAIN. For you, for he has brought Mirabell with him.

FAIN. My dear.

MRS. FAIN. My soul.

FAIN. You don't look well to-day, child.

MRS. FAIN. D'ye think so?

MIRA. He is the only man that does, madam.

MRS. FAIN. The only man that would tell me so at least, and the only man from whom I could hear it without mortification.

FAIN. Oh, my dear, I am satisfied of your tenderness; I know you cannot resent anything from me; especially what is an effect of my concern.

MRS. FAIN. Mr. Mirabell, my mother interrupted you in a pleasant relation last night: I would fain hear it out.

MIRA. The persons concerned in that affair have yet a tolerable reputation. I am afraid Mr. Fainall will be censorious.

MRS. FAIN. He has a humour more prevailing than his curiosity, and will willingly dispense with the hearing of one scandalous story, to avoid giving an occasion to make another by being seen to walk with his wife. This way, Mr. Mirabell, and I dare promise you will oblige us both.

SCENE III.

Fainall, Mrs. Marwood.

FAIN. Excellent creature! Well, sure, if I should live to be rid of my wife, I should be a miserable man.

MRS. MAR. Ay?

FAIN. For having only that one hope, the accomplishment of it of consequence must put an end to all my hopes, and what a wretch is he who must survive his hopes! Nothing remains when that day comes but to sit down and weep like Alexander when he wanted other worlds to conquer.

MRS. MAR. Will you not follow 'em?

FAIN. Faith, I think not,

MRS. MAR. Pray let us; I have a reason.

FAIN. You are not jealous?

MRS. MAR. Of whom?

FAIN. Of Mirabell.

MRS. MAR. If I am, is it inconsistent with my love to you that I am tender of your honour?

FAIN. You would intimate then, as if there were a fellow-feeling between my wife and him?

MRS. MAR. I think she does not hate him to that degree she would be thought.

FAIN. But he, I fear, is too insensible.

MRS. MAR. It may be you are deceived.

FAIN. It may be so. I do not now begin to apprehend it.

MRS. MAR. What?

FAIN. That I have been deceived, madam, and you are false.

MRS. MAR. That I am false? What mean you?

FAIN. To let you know I see through all your little arts.—Come, you both love him, and both have equally dissembled your aversion. Your mutual jealousies of one another have made you clash till you have both struck fire. I have seen the warm confession red'ning on your cheeks, and sparkling from your eyes.

MRS. MAR. You do me wrong.

FAIN. I do not. 'Twas for my ease to oversee and wilfully neglect the gross advances made him by my wife, that by permitting her to be engaged, I might continue unsuspected in my pleasures, and take you oftener to my arms in full security. But could you think, because the nodding husband would not wake, that e'er the watchful lover slept?

MRS. MAR. And wherewithal can you reproach me?

FAIN. With infidelity, with loving another, with love of Mirabell.

MRS. MAR. 'Tis false. I challenge you to show an instance that can confirm your groundless accusation. I hate him.

FAIN. And wherefore do you hate him? He is insensible, and your resentment follows his neglect. An instance? The injuries you have done him are a proof: your interposing in his love. What cause had you to make discoveries of his pretended passion? To undeceive the credulous aunt, and be the officious obstacle of his match with Millamant?

MRS. MAR. My obligations to my lady urged me: I had professed a friendship to her, and could not see her easy nature so abused by that dissembler.

FAIN. What, was it conscience then? Professed a friendship! Oh, the pious friendships of the female sex!

MRS. MAR. More tender, more sincere, and more enduring, than all the vain and empty vows of men, whether professing love to us or mutual faith to one another.

FAIN. Ha, ha, ha! you are my wife's friend too.

MRS. MAR. Shame and ingratitude! Do you reproach me? You, you upbraid me? Have I been false to her, through strict fidelity to you, and sacrificed my friendship to keep my love inviolate? And have you the baseness to charge me with the guilt, unmindful of the merit? To you it should be meritorious that I have been vicious. And do you reflect that guilt upon me which should lie buried in your bosom?

FAIN. You misinterpret my reproof. I meant but to remind you of the slight account you once could make of strictest ties when set in competition with your love to me.

MRS. MAR. 'Tis false, you urged it with deliberate malice. 'Twas spoke in scorn, and I never will forgive it.

FAIN. Your guilt, not your resentment, begets your rage. If yet you loved, you could forgive a jealousy: but you are stung to find you are discovered.

MRS. MAR. It shall be all discovered. You too shall be discovered; be sure you shall. I can but be exposed. If I do it myself I shall prevent your baseness.

FAIN. Why, what will you do?

MRS. MAR. Disclose it to your wife; own what has past between us.

FAIN. Frenzy!

MRS. MAR. By all my wrongs I'll do't. I'll publish to the world the injuries you have done me, both in my fame and fortune: with both I trusted you, you bankrupt in honour, as indigent of wealth.

FAIN. Your fame I have preserved. Your fortune has been bestowed as the prodigality of your love would have it, in pleasures which we both have shared. Yet, had not you been false I had e'er this repaid it. 'Tis true—had you permitted Mirabell with Millamant to have stolen their marriage, my lady had been incensed beyond all means of reconcilement: Millamant had forfeited the moiety of her fortune, which then would have descended to my wife. And wherefore did I marry but to make lawful prize of a rich widow's wealth, and squander it on love and you?

MRS. MAR. Deceit and frivolous pretence!

FAIN. Death, am I not married? What's pretence? Am I not imprisoned, fettered? Have I not a wife? Nay, a wife that was a widow, a young widow, a handsome widow, and would be again a widow, but that I have a heart of proof, and something of a constitution to bustle through the ways of wedlock and this world. Will you yet be reconciled to truth and me?

MRS. MAR. Impossible. Truth and you are inconsistent.—I hate you, and shall for ever.

FAIN. For loving you?

MRS. MAR. I loathe the name of love after such usage; and next to the guilt with which you would asperse me, I scorn you most. Farewell.

FAIN. Nay, we must not part thus.

MRS. MAR. Let me go.

FAIN. Come, I'm sorry.

MRS. MAR. I care not. Let me go. Break my hands, do—I'd leave 'em to get loose.

FAIN. I would not hurt you for the world. Have I no other hold to keep you here?

MRS. MAR. Well, I have deserved it all.

FAIN. You know I love you.

MRS. MAR. Poor dissembling! Oh, that—well, it is not yet—

FAIN. What? What is it not? What is it not yet? It is not yet too late—

MRS. MAR. No, it is not yet too late—I have that comfort.

FAIN. It is, to love another.

MRS. MAR. But not to loathe, detest, abhor mankind, myself, and the whole treacherous world.

FAIN. Nay, this is extravagance. Come, I ask your pardon. No tears—I was to blame, I could not love you and be easy in my doubts. Pray forbear—I believe you; I'm convinced I've done you wrong; and any way, every way will make amends: I'll hate my wife yet more, damn her, I'll part with her, rob her of all she's worth, and we'll retire somewhere, anywhere, to another world; I'll marry thee—be pacified.—'Sdeath, they come: hide your face, your tears. You have a mask: wear it a moment. This way, this way: be persuaded.

SCENE IV.

Mirabell and Mrs. Fainall.

MRS. FAIN. They are here yet.

MIRA. They are turning into the other walk.

MRS. FAIN. While I only hated my husband, I could bear to see him; but since I have despised him, he's too offensive.

MIRA. Oh, you should hate with prudence.

MRS. FAIN. Yes, for I have loved with indiscretion.

MIRA. You should have just so much disgust for your husband as may be sufficient to make you relish your lover.

MRS. FAIN. You have been the cause that I have loved without bounds, and would you set limits to that aversion of which you have been the occasion? Why did you make me marry this man?

MIRA. Why do we daily commit disagreeable and dangerous actions? To save that idol, reputation. If the familiarities of our loves had produced that consequence of which you were apprehensive, where could you have fixed a father's name with credit but on a husband? I knew Fainall to be a man lavish of his morals, an interested and professing friend, a false and a designing lover, yet one whose wit and outward fair behaviour have gained a reputation with the town, enough to make that woman stand excused who has suffered herself to be won by his addresses. A better man ought not to have been sacrificed to the occasion; a worse had not answered to the purpose. When you are weary of him you know your remedy.

MRS. FAIN. I ought to stand in some degree of credit with you, Mirabell.

MIRA. In justice to you, I have made you privy to my whole design, and put it in your power to ruin or advance my fortune.

MRS. FAIN. Whom have you instructed to represent your pretended uncle?

MIRA. Waitwell, my servant.

MRS. FAIN. He is an humble servant to Foible, my mother's woman, and may win her to your interest.

MIRA. Care is taken for that. She is won and worn by this time. They were married this morning.

MRS. FAIN. Who?

MIRA. Waitwell and Foible. I would not tempt my servant to betray me by trusting him too far. If your mother, in hopes to ruin me, should consent to marry my pretended uncle, he might, like Mosca in the Fox, stand upon terms; so I made him sure beforehand.

MRS. FAIN. So, if my poor mother is caught in a contract, you will discover the imposture betimes, and release her by producing a certificate of her gallant's former marriage.

MIRA. Yes, upon condition that she consent to my marriage with her niece, and surrender the moiety of her fortune in her possession.

MRS. FAIN. She talked last night of endeavouring at a match between Millamant and your uncle.

MIRA. That was by Foible's direction and my instruction, that she might seem to carry it more privately.

MRS. FAIN. Well, I have an opinion of your success, for I believe my lady will do anything to get an husband; and when she has this, which you have provided for her, I suppose she will submit to anything to get rid of him.

MIRA. Yes, I think the good lady would marry anything that resembled a man, though 'twere no more than what a butler could pinch out of a napkin.

MRS. FAIN. Female frailty! We must all come to it, if we live to be old, and feel the craving of a false appetite when the true is decayed.

MIRA. An old woman's appetite is depraved like that of a girl. 'Tis the green-sickness of a second childhood, and, like the faint offer of a latter spring, serves but to usher in the fall, and withers in an affected bloom.

MRS. FAIN. Here's your mistress.

SCENE V.

[To them] Mrs. Millamant, Witwoud, Mincing.

MIRA. Here she comes, i'faith, full sail, with her fan spread and streamers out, and a shoal of fools for tenders.—Ha, no, I cry her mercy.

MRS. FAIN. I see but one poor empty sculler, and he tows her woman after him.

MIRA. You seem to be unattended, madam. You used to have the beau monde throng after you, and a flock of gay fine perukes hovering round you.

WIT. Like moths about a candle. I had like to have lost my comparison for want of breath.

MILLA. Oh, I have denied myself airs to-day. I have walked as fast through the crowd—

WIT. As a favourite just disgraced, and with as few followers.

MILLA. Dear Mr. Witwoud, truce with your similitudes, for I am as sick of 'em—

WIT. As a physician of a good air. I cannot help it, madam, though 'tis against myself.

MILLA. Yet again! Mincing, stand between me and his wit.

WIT. Do, Mrs. Mincing, like a screen before a great fire. I confess I do blaze to-day; I am too bright.

MRS. FAIN. But, dear Millamant, why were you so long?

MILLA. Long! Lord, have I not made violent haste? I have asked every living thing I met for you; I have enquired after you, as after a new fashion.

WIT. Madam, truce with your similitudes.—No, you met her husband, and did not ask him for her.

MIRA. By your leave, Witwoud, that were like enquiring after an old fashion to ask a husband for his wife.

WIT. Hum, a hit, a hit, a palpable hit; I confess it.

MRS. FAIN. You were dressed before I came abroad.

MILLA. Ay, that's true. Oh, but then I had—Mincing, what had I? Why was I so long?

MINC. O mem, your laship stayed to peruse a packet of letters.

MILLA. Oh, ay, letters—I had letters—I am persecuted with letters—I hate letters. Nobody knows how to write letters; and yet one has 'em, one does not know why. They serve one to pin up one's hair.

WIT. Is that the way? Pray, madam, do you pin up your hair with all your letters? I find I must keep copies.

MILLA. Only with those in verse, Mr. Witwoud. I never pin up my hair with prose. I think I tried once, Mincing.

MINC. O mem, I shall never forget it.

MILLA. Ay, poor Mincing tift and tift all the morning.

MINC. Till I had the cramp in my fingers, I'll vow, mem. And all to no purpose. But when your laship pins it up with poetry, it fits so pleasant the next day as anything, and is so pure and so crips.

WIT. Indeed, so crips?

MINC. You're such a critic, Mr. Witwoud.

MILLA. Mirabell, did you take exceptions last night? Oh, ay, and went away. Now I think on't I'm angry—no, now I think on't I'm pleased:—for I believe I gave you some pain.

MIRA. Does that please you?

MILLA. Infinitely; I love to give pain.

MIRA. You would affect a cruelty which is not in your nature; your true vanity is in the power of pleasing.

MILLA. Oh, I ask your pardon for that. One's cruelty is one's power, and when one parts with one's cruelty one parts with one's power, and when one has parted with that, I fancy one's old and ugly.

MIRA. Ay, ay; suffer your cruelty to ruin the object of your power, to destroy your lover—and then how vain, how lost a thing you'll be! Nay, 'tis true; you are no longer handsome when you've lost your lover: your beauty dies upon the instant. For beauty is the lover's gift: 'tis he bestows your charms:—your glass is all a cheat. The ugly and the old, whom the looking-glass mortifies, yet after commendation can be flattered by it, and discover beauties in it: for that reflects our praises rather than your face.

MILLA. Oh, the vanity of these men! Fainall, d'ye hear him? If they did not commend us, we were not handsome! Now you must know they could not commend one if one was not handsome. Beauty the lover's gift! Lord, what is a lover, that it can give? Why, one makes lovers as fast as one pleases, and they live as long as one pleases, and they die as soon as one pleases; and then, if one pleases, one makes more.

WIT. Very pretty. Why, you make no more of making of lovers, madam, than of making so many card-matches.

MILLA. One no more owes one's beauty to a lover than one's wit to an echo. They can but reflect what we look and say: vain empty things if we are silent or unseen, and want a being.

MIRA. Yet, to those two vain empty things, you owe two the greatest pleasures of your life.

MILLA. How so?

MIRA. To your lover you owe the pleasure of hearing yourselves praised, and to an echo the pleasure of hearing yourselves talk.

WIT. But I know a lady that loves talking so incessantly, she won't give an echo fair play; she has that everlasting rotation of tongue that an echo must wait till she dies before it can catch her last words.

MILLA. Oh, fiction; Fainall, let us leave these men.

MIRA. Draw off Witwoud. [Aside to Mrs. Fainall.]

MRS. FAIN. Immediately; I have a word or two for Mr. Witwoud.

SCENE VI.

Mrs. Millamant, Mirabell, Mincing.

MIRA. I would beg a little private audience too. You had the tyranny to deny me last night, though you knew I came to impart a secret to you that concerned my love.

MILLA. You saw I was engaged.

MIRA. Unkind! You had the leisure to entertain a herd of fools: things who visit you from their excessive idleness, bestowing on your easiness that time which is the incumbrance of their lives. How can you find delight in such society? It is impossible they should admire you; they are not capable; or, if they were, it should be to you as a mortification: for, sure, to please a fool is some degree of folly.

MILLA. I please myself.—Besides, sometimes to converse with fools is for my health.

MIRA. Your health! Is there a worse disease than the conversation of fools?

MILLA. Yes, the vapours; fools are physic for it, next to assafoetida.

MIRA. You are not in a course of fools?

MILLA. Mirabell, if you persist in this offensive freedom you'll displease me. I think I must resolve after all not to have you:—we shan't agree.

MIRA. Not in our physic, it may be.

MILLA. And yet our distemper in all likelihood will be the same; for we shall be sick of one another. I shan't endure to be reprimanded nor instructed; 'tis so dull to act always by advice, and so tedious to be told of one's faults, I can't bear it. Well, I won't have you, Mirabell—I'm resolved—I think—you may go—ha, ha, ha! What would you give that you could help loving me?

MIRA. I would give something that you did not know I could not help it.

MILLA. Come, don't look grave then. Well, what do you say to me?

MIRA. I say that a man may as soon make a friend by his wit, or a fortune by his honesty, as win a woman with plain-dealing and sincerity.

MILLA. Sententious Mirabell! Prithee don't look with that violent and inflexible wise face, like Solomon at the dividing of the child in an old tapestry hanging!

MIRA. You are merry, madam, but I would persuade you for a moment to be serious.

MILLA. What, with that face? No, if you keep your countenance, 'tis impossible I should hold mine. Well, after all, there is something very moving in a lovesick face. Ha, ha, ha! Well I won't laugh; don't be peevish. Heigho! Now I'll be melancholy, as melancholy as a watch-light. Well, Mirabell, if ever you will win me, woo me now.—Nay, if you are so tedious, fare you well: I see they are walking away.

MIRA. Can you not find in the variety of your disposition one moment—

MILLA. To hear you tell me Foible's married, and your plot like to speed? No.

MIRA. But how you came to know it—

MILLA. Without the help of the devil, you can't imagine; unless she should tell me herself. Which of the two it may have been, I will leave you to consider; and when you have done thinking of that, think of me.

SCENE VII.

Mirabell alone.

MIRA. I have something more.—Gone! Think of you? To think of a whirlwind, though 'twere in a whirlwind, were a case of more steady contemplation, a very tranquillity of mind and mansion. A fellow that lives in a windmill has not a more whimsical dwelling than the heart of a man that is lodged in a woman. There is no point of the compass to which they cannot turn, and by which they are not turned, and by one as well as another; for motion, not method, is their occupation. To know this, and yet continue to be in love, is to be made wise from the dictates of reason, and yet persevere to play the fool by the force of instinct.—Oh, here come my pair of turtles. What, billing so sweetly? Is not Valentine's day over with you yet?

SCENE VIII.

[To him] Waitwell, Foible.

MIRA. Sirrah, Waitwell, why, sure, you think you were married for your own recreation and not for my conveniency.

WAIT. Your pardon, sir. With submission, we have indeed been solacing in lawful delights; but still with an eye to business, sir. I have instructed her as well as I could. If she can take your directions as readily as my instructions, sir, your affairs are in a prosperous way.

MIRA. Give you joy, Mrs. Foible.

FOIB. O—las, sir, I'm so ashamed.—I'm afraid my lady has been in a thousand inquietudes for me. But I protest, sir, I made as much haste as I could.

WAIT. That she did indeed, sir. It was my fault that she did not make more.

MIRA. That I believe.

FOIB. But I told my lady as you instructed me, sir, that I had a prospect of seeing Sir Rowland, your uncle, and that I would put her ladyship's picture in my pocket to show him, which I'll be sure to say has made him so enamoured of her beauty, that he burns with impatience to lie at her ladyship's feet and worship the original.

MIRA. Excellent Foible! Matrimony has made you eloquent in love.

WAIT. I think she has profited, sir. I think so.

FOIB. You have seen Madam Millamant, sir?

MIRA. Yes.

FOIB. I told her, sir, because I did not know that you might find an opportunity; she had so much company last night.

MIRA. Your diligence will merit more. In the meantime—[gives money]

FOIB. O dear sir, your humble servant.

WAIT. Spouse—

MIRA. Stand off, sir, not a penny. Go on and prosper, Foible. The lease shall be made good and the farm stocked, if we succeed.

FOIB. I don't question your generosity, sir, and you need not doubt of success. If you have no more commands, sir, I'll be gone; I'm sure my lady is at her toilet, and can't dress till I come. Oh dear, I'm sure that [looking out] was Mrs. Marwood that went by in a mask; if she has seen me with you I'm sure she'll tell my lady. I'll make haste home and prevent her. Your servant, Sir.—B'w'y, Waitwell.

SCENE IX.

Mirabell, Waitwell.

WAIT. Sir Rowland, if you please. The jade's so pert upon her preferment she forgets herself.

MIRA. Come, sir, will you endeavour to forget yourself—and transform into Sir Rowland?

WAIT. Why, sir, it will be impossible I should remember myself. Married, knighted, and attended all in one day! 'Tis enough to make any man forget himself. The difficulty will be how to recover my acquaintance and familiarity with my former self, and fall from my transformation to a reformation into Waitwell. Nay, I shan't be quite the same Waitwell neither—for now I remember me, I'm married, and can't be my own man again.

Ay, there's my grief; that's the sad change of life:
To lose my title, and yet keep my wife.

ACT III. – SCENE I.

A room in Lady Wishfort's house.

Lady Wishfort at her toilet, Peg waiting.

LADY. Merciful! No news of Foible yet?

PEG. No, madam.

LADY. I have no more patience. If I have not fretted myself till I am pale again, there's no veracity in me. Fetch me the red—the red, do you hear, sweetheart? An errant ash colour, as I'm a person. Look you how this wench stirs! Why dost thou not fetch me a little red? Didst thou not hear me, Mopus?

PEG. The red ratafia, does your ladyship mean, or the cherry brandy?

LADY. Ratafia, fool? No, fool. Not the ratafia, fool—grant me patience!—I mean the Spanish paper, idiot; complexion, darling. Paint, paint, paint, dost thou understand that, changeling, dangling thy hands like bobbins before thee? Why dost thou not stir, puppet? Thou wooden thing upon wires!

PEG. Lord, madam, your ladyship is so impatient.—I cannot come at the paint, madam: Mrs. Foible has locked it up, and carried the key with her.

LADY. A pox take you both.—Fetch me the cherry brandy then.

SCENE II.

Lady Wishfort.

I'm as pale and as faint, I look like Mrs. Qualmsick, the curate's wife, that's always breeding. Wench, come, come, wench, what art thou doing? Sipping? Tasting? Save thee, dost thou not know the bottle?

SCENE III.

Lady Wishfort, Peg with a bottle and china cup.

PEG. Madam, I was looking for a cup.

LADY. A cup, save thee, and what a cup hast thou brought! Dost thou take me for a fairy, to drink out of an acorn? Why didst thou not bring thy thimble? Hast thou ne'er a brass thimble clinking in thy pocket with a bit of nutmeg? I warrant thee. Come, fill, fill. So, again. See who that is. [One knocks.] Set down the bottle first. Here, here, under the table:—what, wouldst thou go with the bottle in thy hand like a tapster? As I'm a person, this wench has lived in an inn upon the road, before she came to me, like Maritornes the Asturian in Don Quixote. No Foible yet?

PEG. No, madam; Mrs. Marwood.

LADY. Oh, Marwood: let her come in. Come in, good Marwood.

SCENE IV.

[To them] Mrs. Marwood.

MRS. MAR. I'm surprised to find your ladyship in déshabillé at this time of day.

LADY. Foible's a lost thing; has been abroad since morning, and never heard of since.

MRS. MAR. I saw her but now, as I came masked through the park, in conference with Mirabell.

LADY. With Mirabell? You call my blood into my face with mentioning that traitor. She durst not have the confidence. I sent her to negotiate an affair, in which if I'm detected I'm undone. If that wheedling villain has wrought upon Foible to detect me, I'm ruined. O my dear friend, I'm a wretch of wretches if I'm detected.

MRS. MAR. O madam, you cannot suspect Mrs. Foible's integrity.

LADY. Oh, he carries poison in his tongue that would corrupt integrity itself. If she has given him an opportunity, she has as good as put her integrity into his hands. Ah, dear Marwood, what's integrity to an opportunity? Hark! I hear her. Dear friend, retire into my closet, that I may examine her with more freedom—you'll pardon me, dear friend, I can make bold with you—there are books over the chimney—Quarles and Pryn, and the Short View of the Stage, with Bunyan's works to entertain you.—Go, you thing, and send her in. [To Peg.]

SCENE V.

Lady Wishfort, Foible.

LADY. O Foible, where hast thou been? What hast thou been doing?

FOIB. Madam, I have seen the party.

LADY. But what hast thou done?

FOIB. Nay, 'tis your ladyship has done, and are to do; I have only promised. But a man so enamoured—so transported! Well, if worshipping of pictures be a sin—poor Sir Rowland, I say.

LADY. The miniature has been counted like. But hast thou not betrayed me, Foible? Hast thou not detected me to that faithless Mirabell? What hast thou to do with him in the park? Answer me, has he got nothing out of thee?

FOIB. So, the devil has been beforehand with me; what shall I say?—Alas, madam, could I help it, if I met that confident thing? Was I in fault? If you had heard how he used me, and all upon your ladyship's account, I'm sure you would not suspect my fidelity. Nay, if that had been the worst I could have borne: but he had a fling at your ladyship too, and then I could not hold; but, i'faith I gave him his own.

LADY. Me? What did the filthy fellow say?

FOIB. O madam, 'tis a shame to say what he said, with his taunts and his fleers, tossing up his nose. Humh, says he, what, you are a-hatching some plot, says he, you are so early abroad, or catering, says he, ferreting for some disbanded officer, I warrant. Half pay is but thin subsistence, says he. Well, what pension does your lady propose? Let me see, says he, what, she must come down pretty deep now, she's superannuated, says he, and—

LADY. Ods my life, I'll have him—I'll have him murdered. I'll have him poisoned. Where does he eat? I'll marry a drawer to have him poisoned in his wine. I'll send for Robin from Locket's—immediately.

FOIB. Poison him? Poisoning's too good for him. Starve him, madam, starve him; marry Sir Rowland, and get him disinherited. Oh, you would bless yourself to hear what he said.

LADY. A villain; superannuated?

FOIB. Humh, says he, I hear you are laying designs against me too, says he, and Mrs. Millamant is to marry my uncle (he does not suspect a word of your ladyship); but, says he, I'll fit you for that, I warrant you, says he, I'll hamper you for that, says he, you and your old frippery too, says he, I'll handle you—

LADY. Audacious villain! Handle me? Would he durst? Frippery? Old frippery? Was there ever such a foul-mouthed fellow? I'll be married to-morrow, I'll be contracted to-night.

FOIB. The sooner the better, madam.

LADY. Will Sir Rowland be here, say'st thou? When, Foible?

FOIB. Incontinently, madam. No new sheriff's wife expects the return of her husband after knighthood with that impatience in which Sir Rowland burns for the dear hour of kissing your ladyship's hand after dinner.

LADY. Frippery? Superannuated frippery? I'll frippery the villain; I'll reduce him to frippery and rags, a tatterdemalion!—I hope to see him hung with tatters, like a Long Lane pent-house, or a gibbet thief. A slander-mouthed railer! I warrant the spendthrift prodigal's in debt as much as the million lottery, or the whole court upon a birthday. I'll spoil his credit with his tailor. Yes, he shall have my niece with her fortune, he shall.

FOIB. He? I hope to see him lodge in Ludgate first, and angle into Blackfriars for brass farthings with an old mitten.

LADY. Ay, dear Foible; thank thee for that, dear Foible. He has put me out of all patience. I shall never recompose my features to receive Sir Rowland with any economy of face. This wretch has fretted me that I am absolutely decayed. Look, Foible.

FOIB. Your ladyship has frowned a little too rashly, indeed, madam. There are some cracks discernible in the white vernish.

LADY. Let me see the glass. Cracks, say'st thou? Why, I am arrantly flayed: I look like an old peeled wall. Thou must repair me, Foible, before Sir Rowland comes, or I shall never keep up to my picture.

FOIB. I warrant you, madam: a little art once made your picture like you, and now a little of the same art must make you like your picture. Your picture must sit for you, madam.

LADY. But art thou sure Sir Rowland will not fail to come? Or will a not fail when he does come? Will he be importunate, Foible, and push? For if he should not be importunate I shall never break decorums. I shall die with confusion if I am forced to advance—oh no, I can never advance; I shall swoon if he should expect advances. No, I hope Sir Rowland is better bred than to put a lady to the necessity of breaking her forms. I won't be too coy neither—I won't give him despair. But a little disdain is not amiss; a little scorn is alluring.

FOIB. A little scorn becomes your ladyship.

LADY. Yes, but tenderness becomes me best—a sort of a dyingness. You see that picture has a sort of a—ha, Foible? A swimmingness in the eyes. Yes, I'll look so. My niece affects it; but she wants features. Is Sir Rowland handsome? Let my toilet be removed—I'll dress above. I'll receive Sir Rowland here. Is he handsome? Don't answer me. I won't know; I'll be surprised. I'll be taken by surprise.

FOIB. By storm, madam. Sir Rowland's a brisk man.

LADY. Is he? Oh, then, he'll importune, if he's a brisk man. I shall save decorums if Sir Rowland importunes. I have a mortal terror at the apprehension of offending against decorums. Oh, I'm glad he's a brisk man. Let my things be removed, good Foible.

SCENE VI.

Mrs. Fainall, Foible.

MRS. FAIN. O Foible, I have been in a fright, lest I should come too late. That devil, Marwood, saw you in the park with Mirabell, and I'm afraid will discover it to my lady.

FOIB. Discover what, madam?

MRS. FAIN. Nay, nay, put not on that strange face. I am privy to the whole design, and know that Waitwell, to whom thou wert this morning married, is to personate Mirabell's uncle, and, as such winning my lady, to involve her in those difficulties from which Mirabell only must release her, by his making his conditions to have my cousin and her fortune left to her own disposal.

FOIB. O dear madam, I beg your pardon. It was not my confidence in your ladyship that was deficient; but I thought the former good correspondence between your ladyship and Mr. Mirabell might have hindered his communicating this secret.

MRS. FAIN. Dear Foible, forget that.

FOIB. O dear madam, Mr. Mirabell is such a sweet winning gentleman. But your ladyship is the pattern of generosity. Sweet lady, to be so good! Mr. Mirabell cannot choose but be grateful. I find your ladyship has his heart still. Now, madam, I can safely tell your ladyship our success: Mrs. Marwood had told my lady, but I warrant I managed myself. I turned it all for the better. I told my lady that Mr. Mirabell railed at her. I laid horrid things to his charge, I'll vow; and my lady is so incensed that she'll be contracted to Sir Rowland to-night, she says; I warrant I worked her up that he may have her for asking for, as they say of a Welsh maidenhead.

MRS. FAIN. O rare Foible!

FOIB. Madam, I beg your ladyship to acquaint Mr. Mirabell of his success. I would be seen as little as possible to speak to him—besides, I believe Madam Marwood watches me. She has a month's mind; but I know Mr. Mirabell can't abide her. [Calls.] John, remove my lady's toilet. Madam, your servant. My lady is so impatient, I fear she'll come for me, if I stay.

MRS. FAIN. I'll go with you up the back stairs, lest I should meet her.

SCENE VII.

Mrs. Marwood alone.

MRS. MAR. Indeed, Mrs. Engine, is it thus with you? Are you become a go-between of this importance? Yes, I shall watch you. Why this wench is the passe-partout, a very master-key to everybody's strong box. My friend Fainall, have you carried it so swimmingly? I thought there was something in it; but it seems it's over with you. Your loathing is not from a want of appetite then, but from a surfeit. Else you could never be so cool to fall from a principal to be an assistant, to procure for him! A pattern of generosity, that I confess. Well, Mr. Fainall, you have met with your match.—O man, man! Woman, woman! The devil's an ass: if I were a painter, I would draw him like an idiot, a driveller with a bib and bells. Man should have his head and horns, and woman the rest of him. Poor, simple fiend! 'Madam Marwood has a month's mind, but he can't abide her.' 'Twere better for him you had not been his confessor in that affair, without you could have kept his counsel closer. I shall not prove another pattern of generosity; he has not obliged me to that with those excesses of himself, and now I'll have none of him. Here comes the good lady, panting ripe, with a heart full of hope, and a head full of care, like any chymist upon the day of projection.

SCENE VIII.

[To her] Lady Wishfort.

LADY. O dear Marwood, what shall I say for this rude forgetfulness? But my dear friend is all goodness.

MRS. MAR. No apologies, dear madam. I have been very well entertained.

LADY. As I'm a person, I am in a very chaos to think I should so forget myself. But I have such an olio of affairs, really I know not what to do. [Calls.] Foible!—I expect my nephew Sir Wilfull ev'ry moment too.—Why, Foible!—He means to travel for improvement.

MRS. MAR. Methinks Sir Wilfull should rather think of marrying than travelling at his years. I hear he is turned of forty.

LADY. Oh, he's in less danger of being spoiled by his travels. I am against my nephew's marrying too young. It will be time enough when he comes back, and has acquired discretion to choose for himself.

MRS. MAR. Methinks Mrs. Millamant and he would make a very fit match. He may travel afterwards. 'Tis a thing very usual with young gentlemen.

LADY. I promise you I have thought on't—and since 'tis your judgment, I'll think on't again. I assure you I will; I value your judgment extremely. On my word, I'll propose it.

SCENE IX.

[To them] Foible.

LADY. Come, come, Foible—I had forgot my nephew will be here before dinner—I must make haste.

FOIB. Mr. Witwoud and Mr. Petulant are come to dine with your ladyship.

LADY. Oh dear, I can't appear till I am dressed. Dear Marwood, shall I be free with you again, and beg you to entertain 'em? I'll make all imaginable haste. Dear friend, excuse me.

SCENE X.

Mrs. Marwood, Mrs. Millamant, Mincing.

MILLA. Sure, never anything was so unbred as that odious man. Marwood, your servant.

MRS. MAR. You have a colour; what's the matter?

MILLA. That horrid fellow Petulant has provoked me into a flame—I have broke my fan—Mincing, lend me yours.—Is not all the powder out of my hair?

MRS. MAR. No. What has he done?

MILLA. Nay, he has done nothing; he has only talked. Nay, he has said nothing neither; but he has contradicted everything that has been said. For my part, I thought Witwoud and he would have quarrelled.

MINC. I vow, mem, I thought once they would have fit.

MILLA. Well, 'tis a lamentable thing, I swear, that one has not the liberty of choosing one's acquaintance as one does one's clothes.

MRS. MAR. If we had that liberty, we should be as weary of one set of acquaintance, though never so good, as we are of one suit, though never so fine. A fool and a doily stuff would now and then find days of grace, and be worn for variety.

MILLA. I could consent to wear 'em, if they would wear alike; but fools never wear out. They are such drap de Berri things! Without one could give 'em to one's chambermaid after a day or two.

MRS. MAR. 'Twere better so indeed. Or what think you of the playhouse? A fine gay glossy fool should be given there, like a new masking habit, after the masquerade is over, and we have done with the disguise. For a fool's visit is always a disguise, and never admitted by a woman of wit, but to blind her affair with a lover of sense. If you would but appear barefaced now, and own Mirabell, you might as easily put off Petulant and Witwoud as your hood and scarf. And indeed 'tis time, for the town has found it, the secret is grown too big for the pretence. 'Tis like Mrs. Primly's great belly: she may lace it down before, but it burnishes on her hips. Indeed, Millamant, you can no more conceal it than my Lady Strammel can her face, that goodly face, which in defiance of her Rhenish-wine tea will not be comprehended in a mask.

MILLA. I'll take my death, Marwood, you are more censorious than a decayed beauty, or a discarded toast:—Mincing, tell the men they may come up. My aunt is not dressing here; their folly is less provoking than your malice.

SCENE XI.

Mrs. Millamant, Mrs. Marwood.

MILLA. The town has found it? What has it found? That Mirabell loves me is no more a secret than it is a secret that you discovered it to my aunt, or than the reason why you discovered it is a secret.

MRS. MAR. You are nettled.

MILLA. You're mistaken. Ridiculous!

MRS. MAR. Indeed, my dear, you'll tear another fan, if you don't mitigate those violent airs.

MILLA. O silly! Ha, ha, ha! I could laugh immoderately. Poor Mirabell! His constancy to me has quite destroyed his complaisance for all the world beside. I swear I never enjoined it him to be so coy. If I had the vanity to think he would obey me, I would command him to show more gallantry: 'tis hardly well-bred to be so particular on one hand and so insensible on the other. But I despair to prevail, and so let him follow his own way. Ha, ha, ha! Pardon me, dear creature, I must laugh; ha, ha, ha! Though I grant you 'tis a little barbarous; ha, ha, ha!

MRS. MAR. What pity 'tis so much fine raillery, and delivered with so significant gesture, should be so unhappily directed to miscarry.

MILLA. Heh? Dear creature, I ask your pardon. I swear I did not mind you.

MRS. MAR. Mr. Mirabell and you both may think it a thing impossible, when I shall tell him by telling you—

MILLA. Oh dear, what? For it is the same thing, if I hear it. Ha, ha, ha!

MRS. MAR. That I detest him, hate him, madam.

MILLA. O madam, why, so do I. And yet the creature loves me, ha, ha, ha! How can one forbear laughing to think of it? I am a sibyl if I am not amazed to think what he can see in me. I'll take my death, I think you are handsomer, and within a year or two as young. If you could but stay for me, I should overtake you—but that cannot be. Well, that thought makes me melancholic.—Now I'll be sad.

MRS. MAR. Your merry note may be changed sooner than you think.

MILLA. D'ye say so? Then I'm resolved I'll have a song to keep up my spirits.

SCENE XII.

[To them] Mincing.

MINC. The gentlemen stay but to comb, madam, and will wait on you.

MILLA. Desire Mrs. — that is in the next room, to sing the song I would have learnt yesterday. You shall hear it, madam. Not that there's any great matter in it—but 'tis agreeable to my humour.

SONG.

Set by Mr. John Eccles.

I

Love's but the frailty of the mind
When 'tis not with ambition joined;
A sickly flame, which if not fed expires,
And feeding, wastes in self-consuming fires.

II

'Tis not to wound a wanton boy
Or am'rous youth, that gives the joy;
But 'tis the glory to have pierced a swain
For whom inferior beauties sighed in vain.

III

Then I alone the conquest prize,
When I insult a rival's eyes;
If there's delight in love, 'tis when I see
That heart, which others bleed for, bleed for me.

SCENE XIII.

[To them] Petulant, Witwoud.

MILLA. Is your animosity composed, gentlemen?

WIT. Raillery, raillery, madam; we have no animosity. We hit off a little wit now and then, but no animosity. The falling out of wits is like the falling out of lovers:—we agree in the main, like treble and bass. Ha, Petulant?

PET. Ay, in the main. But when I have a humour to contradict—

WIT. Ay, when he has a humour to contradict, then I contradict too. What, I know my cue. Then we contradict one another like two battledores; for contradictions beget one another like Jews.

PET. If he says black's black—if I have a humour to say 'tis blue—let that pass—all's one for that. If I have a humour to prove it, it must be granted.

WIT. Not positively must. But it may; it may.

PET. Yes, it positively must, upon proof positive.

WIT. Ay, upon proof positive it must; but upon proof presumptive it only may. That's a logical distinction now, madam.

MRS. MAR. I perceive your debates are of importance, and very learnedly handled.

PET. Importance is one thing and learning's another; but a debate's a debate, that I assert.

WIT. Petulant's an enemy to learning; he relies altogether on his parts.

PET. No, I'm no enemy to learning; it hurts not me.

MRS. MAR. That's a sign, indeed, it's no enemy to you.

PET. No, no, it's no enemy to anybody but them that have it.

MILLA. Well, an illiterate man's my aversion; I wonder at the impudence of any illiterate man to offer to make love.

WIT. That I confess I wonder at, too.

MILLA. Ah, to marry an ignorant that can hardly read or write!

PET. Why should a man be any further from being married, though he can't read, than he is from being hanged? The ordinary's paid for setting the psalm, and the parish priest for reading the ceremony. And for the rest which is to follow in both cases, a man may do it without book. So all's one for that.

MILLA. D'ye hear the creature? Lord, here's company; I'll begone.

SCENE XIV.

Sir Wilfull Witwoud in a riding dress, Mrs. Marwood, Petulant, Witwoud, Footman.

WIT. In the name of Bartlemew and his Fair, what have we here?

MRS. MAR. 'Tis your brother, I fancy. Don't you know him?

WIT. Not I:—yes, I think it is he. I've almost forgot him; I have not seen him since the revolution.

FOOT. Sir, my lady's dressing. Here's company, if you please to walk in, in the meantime.

SIR WIL. Dressing! What, it's but morning here, I warrant, with you in London; we should count it towards afternoon in our parts down in Shropshire:—why, then, belike my aunt han't dined yet. Ha, friend?

FOOT. Your aunt, sir?

SIR WIL. My aunt, sir? Yes my aunt, sir, and your lady, sir; your lady is my aunt, sir. Why, what dost thou not know me, friend? Why, then, send somebody hither that does. How long hast thou lived with thy lady, fellow, ha?

FOOT. A week, sir; longer than anybody in the house, except my lady's woman.

SIR WIL. Why, then, belike thou dost not know thy lady, if thou seest her. Ha, friend?

FOOT. Why, truly, sir, I cannot safely swear to her face in a morning, before she is dressed. 'Tis like I may give a shrewd guess at her by this time.

SIR WIL. Well, prithee try what thou canst do; if thou canst not guess, enquire her out, dost hear, fellow? And tell her her nephew, Sir Wilfull Witwoud, is in the house.

FOOT. I shall, sir.

SIR WIL. Hold ye, hear me, friend, a word with you in your ear: prithee who are these gallants?

FOOT. Really, sir, I can't tell; here come so many here, 'tis hard to know 'em all.

SCENE XV.

Sir Wilfull Witwoud, Petulant, Witwoud, Mrs. Marwood.

SIR WIL. Oons, this fellow knows less than a starling: I don't think a knows his own name.

MRS. MAR. Mr. Witwoud, your brother is not behindhand in forgetfulness. I fancy he has forgot you too.

WIT. I hope so. The devil take him that remembers first, I say.

SIR WIL. Save you, gentlemen and lady.

MRS. MAR. For shame, Mr. Witwoud; why won't you speak to him?—And you, sir.

WIT. Petulant, speak.

PET. And you, sir.

SIR WIL. No offence, I hope? [Salutes Marwood.]

MRS. MAR. No, sure, sir.

WIT. This is a vile dog, I see that already. No offence? Ha, ha, ha. To him, to him, Petulant, smoke him.

PET. It seems as if you had come a journey, sir; hem, hem. [Surveying him round.]

SIR WIL. Very likely, sir, that it may seem so.

PET. No offence, I hope, sir?

WIT. Smoke the boots, the boots, Petulant, the boots; ha, ha, ha!

SIR WILL. Maybe not, sir; thereafter as 'tis meant, sir.

PET. Sir, I presume upon the information of your boots.

SIR WIL. Why, 'tis like you may, sir: if you are not satisfied with the information of my boots, sir, if you will step to the stable, you may enquire further of my horse, sir.

PET. Your horse, sir! Your horse is an ass, sir!

SIR WIL. Do you speak by way of offence, sir?

MRS. MAR. The gentleman's merry, that's all, sir. 'Slife, we shall have a quarrel betwixt an horse and an ass, before they find one another out.—You must not take anything amiss from your friends, sir. You are among your friends here, though it—may be you don't know it. If I am not mistaken, you are Sir Wilfull Witwoud?

SIR WIL. Right, lady; I am Sir Wilfull Witwoud, so I write myself; no offence to anybody, I hope? and nephew to the Lady Wishfort of this mansion.

MRS. MAR. Don't you know this gentleman, sir?

SIR WIL. Hum! What, sure 'tis not—yea by'r lady but 'tis—'sheart, I know not whether 'tis or no. Yea, but 'tis, by the Wrekin. Brother

Antony! What, Tony, i'faith! What, dost thou not know me? By'r lady, nor I thee, thou art so becravated and so beperiwigged. 'Sheart, why dost not speak? Art thou o'erjoyed?

WIT. Odso, brother, is it you? Your servant, brother.

SIR WIL. Your servant? Why, yours, sir. Your servant again—'sheart, and your friend and servant to that—and a—[puff] and a flap-dragon for your service, sir, and a hare's foot and a hare's scut for your service, sir, an you be so cold and so courtly!

WIT. No offence, I hope, brother?

SIR WIL. 'Sheart, sir, but there is, and much offence. A pox, is this your inns o' court breeding, not to know your friends and your relations, your elders, and your betters?

WIT. Why, brother Wilfull of Salop, you may be as short as a Shrewsbury cake, if you please. But I tell you 'tis not modish to know relations in town. You think you're in the country, where great lubberly brothers slabber and kiss one another when they meet, like a call of sergeants. 'Tis not the fashion here; 'tis not, indeed, dear brother.

SIR WIL. The fashion's a fool and you're a fop, dear brother. 'Sheart, I've suspected this—by'r lady I conjectured you were a fop, since you began to change the style of your letters, and write in a scrap of paper gilt round the edges, no bigger than a subpoena. I might expect this when you left off 'Honoured brother,' and 'Hoping you are in good health,' and so forth, to begin with a 'Rat me, knight, I'm so sick of a last night's debauch.' Ods heart, and then tell a familiar tale of a cock and a bull, and a whore and a bottle, and so conclude. You could write news before you were out of your time, when you lived with honest Pumple-Nose, the attorney of Furnival's Inn. You could intreat to be remembered then to your friends round the Wrekin. We could have Gazettes then, and Dawks's Letter, and the Weekly Bill, till of late days.

PET. 'Slife, Witwoud, were you ever an attorney's clerk? Of the family of the Furnivals? Ha, ha, ha!

WIT. Ay, ay, but that was but for a while. Not long, not long; pshaw, I was not in my own power then. An orphan, and this fellow was my guardian; ay, ay, I was glad to consent to that man to come to London. He had the disposal of me then. If I had not agreed to that, I might have been bound prentice to a feltmaker in Shrewsbury: this fellow would have bound me to a maker of felts.

SIR WIL. 'Sheart, and better than to be bound to a maker of fops, where, I suppose, you have served your time, and now you may set up for yourself.

MRS. MAR. You intend to travel, sir, as I'm informed?

SIR WIL. Belike I may, madam. I may chance to sail upon the salt seas, if my mind hold.

PET. And the wind serve.

SIR WIL. Serve or not serve, I shan't ask license of you, sir, nor the weathercock your companion. I direct my discourse to the lady, sir. 'Tis like my aunt may have told you, madam? Yes, I have settled my concerns, I may say now, and am minded to see foreign parts. If an how that the peace holds, whereby, that is, taxes abate.

MRS. MAR. I thought you had designed for France at all adventures.

SIR WIL. I can't tell that; 'tis like I may, and 'tis like I may not. I am somewhat dainty in making a resolution, because when I make it I keep it. I don't stand shill I, shall I, then; if I say't, I'll do't. But I have thoughts to tarry a small matter in town, to learn somewhat of your lingo first, before I cross the seas. I'd gladly have a spice of your French as they say, whereby to hold discourse in foreign countries.

MRS. MAR. Here's an academy in town for that use.

SIR WIL. There is? 'Tis like there may.

MRS. MAR. No doubt you will return very much improved.

WIT. Yes, refined like a Dutch skipper from a whale-fishing.

SCENE XVI.

[To them] Lady Wishfort and Fainall.

LADY. Nephew, you are welcome.

SIR WIL. Aunt, your servant.

FAIN. Sir Wilfull, your most faithful servant.

SIR WIL. Cousin Fainall, give me your hand.

LADY. Cousin Witwoud, your servant; Mr. Petulant, your servant. Nephew, you are welcome again. Will you drink anything after your journey, nephew, before you eat? Dinner's almost ready.

SIR WIL. I'm very well, I thank you, aunt. However, I thank you for your courteous offer. 'Sheart, I was afraid you would have been in the fashion too, and have remembered to have forgot your relations. Here's your cousin Tony, belike, I mayn't call him brother for fear of offence.

LADY. Oh, he's a rallier, nephew. My cousin's a wit: and your great wits always rally their best friends to choose. When you have been abroad, nephew, you'll understand raillery better. [Fainall and Mrs. Marwood talk apart.]

SIR WIL. Why, then, let him hold his tongue in the meantime, and rail when that day comes.

SCENE XVII.

[To them] Mincing.

MINC. Mem, I come to acquaint your laship that dinner is impatient.

SIR WIL. Impatient? Why, then, belike it won't stay till I pull off my boots. Sweetheart, can you help me to a pair of slippers? My man's with his horses, I warrant.

LADY. Fie, fie, nephew, you would not pull off your boots here? Go down into the hall:—dinner shall stay for you. My nephew's a little unbred: you'll pardon him, madam. Gentlemen, will you walk? Marwood?

MRS. MAR. I'll follow you, madam,—before Sir Wilfull is ready.

SCENE XVIII.

Mrs. Marwood, Fainall.

FAIN. Why, then, Foible's a bawd, an errant, rank match-making bawd. And I, it seems, am a husband, a rank husband, and my wife a very errant, rank wife,—all in the way of the world. 'Sdeath, to be a cuckold by anticipation, a cuckold in embryo! Sure I was born with budding antlers like a young satyr, or a citizen's child, 'sdeath, to be outwitted, to be out-jilted, out-matrimonied. If I had kept my speed like a stag, 'twere somewhat, but to crawl after, with my horns like a snail, and be outstripped by my wife—'tis scurvy wedlock.

MRS. MAR. Then shake it off: you have often wished for an opportunity to part, and now you have it. But first prevent their plot:—the half of Millamant's fortune is too considerable to be parted with to a foe, to Mirabell.

FAIN. Damn him, that had been mine—had you not made that fond discovery. That had been forfeited, had they been married. My wife had added lustre to my horns by that increase of fortune: I could have worn 'em tipt with gold, though my forehead had been furnished like a deputy-lieutenant's hall.

MRS. MAR. They may prove a cap of maintenance to you still, if you can away with your wife. And she's no worse than when you had her:—I dare swear she had given up her game before she was married.

FAIN. Hum! That may be—

MRS. MAR. You married her to keep you; and if you can contrive to have her keep you better than you expected, why should you not keep her longer than you intended?

FAIN. The means, the means?

MRS. MAR. Discover to my lady your wife's conduct; threaten to part with her. My lady loves her, and will come to any composition to save her reputation. Take the opportunity of breaking it just upon the discovery of this imposture. My lady will be enraged beyond bounds, and sacrifice niece, and fortune and all at that conjuncture. And let me alone to keep her warm: if she should flag in her part, I will not fail to prompt her.

FAIN. Faith, this has an appearance.

MRS. MAR. I'm sorry I hinted to my lady to endeavour a match between Millamant and Sir Wilfull; that may be an obstacle.

FAIN. Oh, for that matter, leave me to manage him; I'll disable him for that, he will drink like a Dane. After dinner I'll set his hand in.

MRS. MAR. Well, how do you stand affected towards your lady?

FAIN. Why, faith, I'm thinking of it. Let me see. I am married already; so that's over. My wife has played the jade with me; well, that's over too. I never loved her, or if I had, why that would have been over too by this time. Jealous of her I cannot be, for I am certain; so there's an end of jealousy. Weary of her I am and shall be. No, there's no end of that; no, no, that were too much to hope. Thus far concerning my repose. Now for my reputation: as to my own, I married not for it; so that's out of the question. And as to my part in my wife's—why, she had parted with hers before; so, bringing none to me, she can take none from me: 'tis against all rule of play that I should lose to one who has not wherewithal to stake.

MRS. MAR. Besides you forget, marriage is honourable.

FAIN. Hum! Faith, and that's well thought on: marriage is honourable, as you say; and if so, wherefore should cuckoldom be a discredit, being derived from so honourable a root?

MRS. MAR. Nay, I know not; if the root be honourable, why not the branches?

FAIN. So, so; why this point's clear. Well, how do we proceed?

MRS. MAR. I will contrive a letter which shall be delivered to my lady at the time when that rascal who is to act Sir Rowland is with her. It shall come as from an unknown hand—for the less I appear to know of the truth the better I can play the incendiary. Besides, I would not have Foible provoked if I could help it, because, you know, she knows some passages. Nay, I expect all will come out. But let the mine be sprung first, and then I care not if I am discovered.

FAIN. If the worst come to the worst, I'll turn my wife to grass. I have already a deed of settlement of the best part of her estate, which I wheedled out of her, and that you shall partake at least.

MRS. MAR. I hope you are convinced that I hate Mirabell now? You'll be no more jealous?

FAIN. Jealous? No, by this kiss. Let husbands be jealous, but let the lover still believe: or if he doubt, let it be only to endear his pleasure, and prepare the joy that follows, when he proves his mistress true. But let husbands' doubts convert to endless jealousy; or if they have belief, let it corrupt to superstition and blind credulity. I am single and will herd no more with 'em. True, I wear the badge, but I'll disown the order. And since I take my leave of 'em, I care not if I leave 'em a common motto to their common crest.

All husbands must or pain or shame endure;

The wise too jealous are, fools too secure.

ACT IV.—SCENE I.

Scene Continues.

Lady Wishfort and Foible.

LADY. Is Sir Rowland coming, say'st thou, Foible? And are things in order?

FOIB. Yes, madam. I have put wax-lights in the sconces, and placed the footmen in a row in the hall, in their best liveries, with the coachman and postillion to fill up the equipage.

LADY. Have you pulvilled the coachman and postillion, that they may not stink of the stable when Sir Rowland comes by?

FOIB. Yes, madam.

LADY. And are the dancers and the music ready, that he may be entertained in all points with correspondence to his passion?

FOIB. All is ready, madam.

LADY. And—well—and how do I look, Foible?

FOIB. Most killing well, madam.

LADY. Well, and how shall I receive him? In what figure shall I give his heart the first impression? There is a great deal in the first impression. Shall I sit? No, I won't sit, I'll walk,—ay, I'll walk from the door upon his entrance, and then turn full upon him. No, that will be too sudden. I'll lie,—ay, I'll lie down. I'll receive him in my little dressing-room; there's a couch—yes, yes, I'll give the first impression on a couch. I won't lie neither, but loll and lean upon one elbow, with one foot a little dangling off, jogging in a thoughtful way. Yes; and then as soon as he appears, start, ay, start and be surprised, and rise to meet him in a pretty disorder. Yes; oh, nothing is more alluring than a levee from a couch in some confusion. It shows the foot to advantage, and furnishes with blushes and re-composing airs beyond comparison. Hark! There's a coach.

FOIB. 'Tis he, madam.

LADY. Oh dear, has my nephew made his addresses to Millamant? I ordered him.

FOIB. Sir Wilfull is set in to drinking, madam, in the parlour.

LADY. Ods my life, I'll send him to her. Call her down, Foible; bring her hither. I'll send him as I go. When they are together, then come to me, Foible, that I may not be too long alone with Sir Rowland.

SCENE II.

Mrs. Millamant, Mrs. Fainall, Foible.

FOIB. Madam, I stayed here to tell your ladyship that Mr. Mirabell has waited this half hour for an opportunity to talk with you; though my lady's orders were to leave you and Sir Wilfull together. Shall I tell Mr. Mirabell that you are at leisure?

MILLA. No. What would the dear man have? I am thoughtful and would amuse myself; bid him come another time.

There never yet was woman made,

Nor shall, but to be cursed.

[Repeating and walking about.]

That's hard!

MRS. FAIN. You are very fond of Sir John Suckling to-day, Millamant, and the poets.

MILLA. He? Ay, and filthy verses. So I am.

FOIB. Sir Wilfull is coming, madam. Shall I send Mr. Mirabell away?

MILLA. Ay, if you please, Foible, send him away, or send him hither, just as you will, dear Foible. I think I'll see him. Shall I? Ay, let the wretch come.

Thyrsis, a youth of the inspired train.

[Repeating]

Dear Fainall, entertain Sir Wilfull:—thou hast philosophy to undergo a fool; thou art married and hast patience. I would confer with my own thoughts.

MRS. FAIN. I am obliged to you that you would make me your proxy in this affair, but I have business of my own.

SCENE III.

[To them] Sir Wilfull.

MRS. FAIN. O Sir Wilfull, you are come at the critical instant. There's your mistress up to the ears in love and contemplation; pursue your point, now or never.

SIR WIL. Yes, my aunt will have it so. I would gladly have been encouraged with a bottle or two, because I'm somewhat wary at first, before I am acquainted. [This while Millamant walks about repeating to herself.] But I hope, after a time, I shall break my mind—that is, upon further acquaintance.—So for the present, cousin, I'll take my leave. If so be you'll be so kind to make my excuse, I'll return to my company—

MRS. FAIN. Oh, fie, Sir Wilfull! What, you must not be daunted.

SIR WIL. Daunted? No, that's not it; it is not so much for that—for if so be that I set on't I'll do't. But only for the present, 'tis sufficient till further acquaintance, that's all—your servant.

MRS. FAIN. Nay, I'll swear you shall never lose so favourable an opportunity, if I can help it. I'll leave you together and lock the door.

SCENE IV.

Sir Wilfull, Millamant.

SIR WIL. Nay, nay, cousin. I have forgot my gloves. What d'ye do? 'Sheart, a has locked the door indeed, I think.—Nay, cousin Fainall, open the door. Pshaw, what a vixen trick is this? Nay, now a has seen me too.—Cousin, I made bold to pass through as it were—I think this door's enchanted.

MILLA. [repeating]:—

I prithee spare me, gentle boy,

Press me no more for that slight toy.

SIR WIL. Anan? Cousin, your servant.

MILLA. That foolish trifle of a heart—

Sir Wilfull!

SIR WIL. Yes—your servant. No offence, I hope, cousin?

MILLA. [repeating]:—

I swear it will not do its part,

Though thou dost thine, employ'st thy power and art.

Natural, easy Suckling!

SIR WIL. Anan? Suckling? No such suckling neither, cousin, nor stripling: I thank heaven I'm no minor.

MILLA. Ah, rustic, ruder than Gothic.

SIR WIL. Well, well, I shall understand your lingo one of these days, cousin; in the meanwhile I must answer in plain English.

MILLA. Have you any business with me, Sir Wilfull?

SIR WIL. Not at present, cousin. Yes, I made bold to see, to come and know if that how you were disposed to fetch a walk this evening; if so be that I might not be troublesome, I would have sought a walk with you.

MILLA. A walk? What then?

SIR WIL. Nay, nothing. Only for the walk's sake, that's all.

MILLA. I nauseate walking: 'tis a country diversion; I loathe the country and everything that relates to it.

SIR WIL. Indeed! Hah! Look ye, look ye, you do? Nay, 'tis like you may. Here are choice of pastimes here in town, as plays and the like, that must be confessed indeed—

MILLA. Ah, l'étourdi! I hate the town too.

SIR WIL. Dear heart, that's much. Hah! that you should hate 'em both! Hah! 'tis like you may! There are some can't relish the town, and others can't away with the country, 'tis like you may be one of those, cousin.

MILLA. Ha, ha, ha! Yes, 'tis like I may. You have nothing further to say to me?

SIR WIL. Not at present, cousin. 'Tis like when I have an opportunity to be more private—I may break my mind in some measure—I conjecture you partly guess. However, that's as time shall try. But spare to speak and spare to speed, as they say.

MILLA. If it is of no great importance, Sir Wilfull, you will oblige me to leave me: I have just now a little business.

SIR WIL. Enough, enough, cousin. Yes, yes, all a case. When you're disposed, when you're disposed. Now's as well as another time; and another time as well as now. All's one for that. Yes, yes; if your concerns call you, there's no haste: it will keep cold as they say. Cousin, your servant. I think this door's locked.

MILLA. You may go this way, sir.

SIR WIL. Your servant; then with your leave I'll return to my company.

MILLA. Ay, ay; ha, ha, ha!

Like Phœbus sung the no less am'rous boy.

SCENE V.

Mrs. Millamant, Mirabell.

MIRA. Like Daphne she, as lovely and as coy.

Do you lock yourself up from me, to make my search more curious? Or is this pretty artifice contrived, to signify that here the chase must end, and my pursuit be crowned, for you can fly no further?

MILLA. Vanity! No—I'll fly and be followed to the last moment; though I am upon the very verge of matrimony, I expect you should solicit me as much as if I were wavering at the grate of a monastery, with one foot over the threshold. I'll be solicited to the very last; nay, and afterwards.

MIRA. What, after the last?

MILLA. Oh, I should think I was poor and had nothing to bestow if I were reduced to an inglorious ease, and freed from the agreeable fatigues of solicitation.

MIRA. But do not you know that when favours are conferred upon instant and tedious solicitation, that they diminish in their value, and that both the giver loses the grace, and the receiver lessens his pleasure?

MILLA. It may be in things of common application, but never, sure, in love. Oh, I hate a lover that can dare to think he draws a moment's air independent on the bounty of his mistress. There is not so impudent a thing in nature as the saucy look of an assured man confident of success: the pedantic arrogance of a very husband has not so pragmatical an air. Ah, I'll never marry, unless I am first made sure of my will and pleasure.

MIRA. Would you have 'em both before marriage? Or will you be contented with the first now, and stay for the other till after grace?

MILLA. Ah, don't be impertinent. My dear liberty, shall I leave thee? My faithful solitude, my darling contemplation, must I bid you then adieu? Ay-h, adieu. My morning thoughts, agreeable wakings, indolent slumbers, all *ye douceurs, ye sommeils du matin*, adieu. I can't do't, 'tis more than impossible—positively, Mirabell, I'll lie a-bed in a morning as long as I please.

MI RA. Then I'll get up in a morning as early as I please.

MILLA. Ah! Idle creature, get up when you will. And d'ye hear, I won't be called names after I'm married; positively I won't be called names.

MIRA. Names?

MILLA. Ay, as wife, spouse, my dear, joy, jewel, love, sweetheart, and the rest of that nauseous cant, in which men and their wives are so fulsomely familiar—I shall never bear that. Good Mirabell, don't let us be familiar or fond, nor kiss before folks, like my Lady Fadler and Sir Francis; nor go to Hyde Park together the first Sunday in a new chariot, to provoke eyes and whispers, and then never be seen there together again, as if we were proud of one another the first week, and ashamed of one another ever after. Let us never visit together, nor go to a play together, but let us be very strange and well-bred. Let us be as strange as if we had been married a great while, and as well-bred as if we were not married at all.

MIRA. Have you any more conditions to offer? Hitherto your demands are pretty reasonable.

MILLA. Trifles; as liberty to pay and receive visits to and from whom I please; to write and receive letters, without interrogatories or wry faces on your part; to wear what I please, and choose conversation with regard only to my own taste; to have no obligation upon me to converse with wits that I don't like, because they are your acquaintance, or to be intimate with fools, because they may be your relations. Come to dinner when I please, dine in my dressing-room when I'm out of humour, without giving a reason. To have my closet inviolate; to be sole empress of my tea-table, which you must never presume to approach without first asking leave. And lastly, wherever I am, you shall always knock at the door before you come in. These articles subscribed, if I continue to endure you a little longer, I may by degrees dwindle into a wife.

MIRA. Your bill of fare is something advanced in this latter account. Well, have I liberty to offer conditions:—that when you are dwindled into a wife, I may not be beyond measure enlarged into a husband?

MILLA. You have free leave: propose your utmost, speak and spare not.

MIRA. I thank you. Imprimis, then, I covenant that your acquaintance be general; that you admit no sworn confidant or intimate of your own sex; no she friend to screen her affairs under your countenance, and tempt you to make trial of a mutual secrecy. No decoy-duck to wheedle you a fop-scrambling to the play in a mask, then bring you home in a pretended fright, when you think you shall be found out, and rail at me for missing the play, and disappointing the frolic which you had to pick me up and prove my constancy.

MILLA. Detestable imprimis! I go to the play in a mask!

MIRA. Item, I article, that you continue to like your own face as long as I shall, and while it passes current with me, that you endeavour not to new coin it. To which end, together with all vizards for the day, I prohibit all masks for the night, made of oiled skins and I know not what—hog's bones, hare's gall, pig water, and the marrow of a roasted cat. In short, I forbid all commerce with the gentlewomen in what-d'ye-call-it court. Item, I shut my doors against all bawds with baskets, and pennyworths of muslin, china, fans, atlases, etc. Item, when you shall be breeding—

MILLA. Ah, name it not!

MIRA. Which may be presumed, with a blessing on our endeavours—

MILLA. Odious endeavours!

MIRA. I denounce against all strait lacing, squeezing for a shape, till you mould my boy's head like a sugar-loaf, and instead of a man-child, make me father to a crooked billet. Lastly, to the dominion of the tea-table I submit; but with proviso, that you exceed not in your province, but restrain yourself to native and simple tea-table drinks, as tea, chocolate, and coffee. As likewise to genuine and authorised tea-table talk, such as mending of fashions, spoiling reputations, railing at absent friends, and so forth. But that on no account you encroach upon the men's prerogative, and presume to drink healths, or toast fellows; for prevention of which, I banish all foreign forces, all auxiliaries to the tea-table, as orange-brandy, all aniseed, cinnamon, citron, and Barbadoes waters, together with ratafia and the most noble spirit of clary. But for cowslip-wine, poppy-water, and all dormitives, those I allow. These provisos admitted, in other things I may prove a tractable and complying husband.

MILLA. Oh, horrid provisos! Filthy strong waters! I toast fellows, odious men! I hate your odious provisos.

MIRA. Then we're agreed. Shall I kiss your hand upon the contract? And here comes one to be a witness to the sealing of the deed.

SCENE VI.

[To them] Mrs. Fainall.

MILLA. Fainall, what shall I do? Shall I have him? I think I must have him.

MRS. FAIN. Ay, ay, take him, take him, what should you do?

MILLA. Well then—I'll take my death I'm in a horrid fright—Fainall, I shall never say it. Well—I think—I'll endure you.

MRS. FAIN. Fie, fie, have him, and tell him so in plain terms: for I am sure you have a mind to him.

MILLA. Are you? I think I have; and the horrid man looks as if he thought so too. Well, you ridiculous thing you, I'll have you. I won't be kissed, nor I won't be thanked.—Here, kiss my hand though, so hold your tongue now; don't say a word.

MRS. FAIN. Mirabell, there's a necessity for your obedience: you have neither time to talk nor stay. My mother is coming; and in my conscience if she should see you, would fall into fits, and maybe not recover time enough to return to Sir Rowland, who, as Foible tells me, is in a fair way to succeed. Therefore spare your ecstasies for another occasion, and slip down the back stairs, where Foible waits to consult you.

MILLA. Ay, go, go. In the meantime I suppose you have said something to please me.

MIRA. I am all obedience.

SCENE VII.

Mrs. Millamant, Mrs. Fainall.

MRS. FAIN. Yonder Sir Wilfull's drunk, and so noisy that my mother has been forced to leave Sir Rowland to appease him; but he answers her only with singing and drinking. What they may have done by this time I know not, but Petulant and he were upon quarrelling as I came by.

MILLA. Well, if Mirabell should not make a good husband, I am a lost thing: for I find I love him violently.

MRS. FAIN. So it seems; for you mind not what's said to you. If you doubt him, you had best take up with Sir Wilfull.

MILLA. How can you name that superannuated lubber? foh!

SCENE VIII.

[To them] Witwoud from drinking.

MRS. FAIN. So, is the fray made up that you have left 'em?

WIT. Left 'em? I could stay no longer. I have laughed like ten

Christ'nings. I am tipsy with laughing—if I had stayed any longer I should have burst,—I must have been let out and pieced in the sides like an unsized camlet. Yes, yes, the fray is composed; my lady came in like a noli prosequi, and stopt the proceedings.

MILLA. What was the dispute?

WIT. That's the jest: there was no dispute. They could neither of 'em speak for rage; and so fell a sputt'ring at one another like two roasting apples.

SCENE IX.

[To them] Petulant drunk.

WIT. Now, Petulant? All's over, all's well? Gad, my head begins to whim it about. Why dost thou not speak? Thou art both as drunk and as mute as a fish.

PET. Look you, Mrs. Millamant, if you can love me, dear Nymph, say it, and that's the conclusion—pass on, or pass off—that's all.

WIT. Thou hast uttered volumes, folios, in less than decimo sexto, my dear Lacedemonian. Sirrah, Petulant, thou art an epitomiser of words.

PET. Witwoud,—you are an annihilator of sense.

WIT. Thou art a retailer of phrases, and dost deal in remnants of remnants, like a maker of pincushions; thou art in truth (metaphorically speaking) a speaker of shorthand.

PET. Thou art (without a figure) just one half of an ass, and Baldwin yonder, thy half-brother, is the rest. A Gemini of asses split would make just four of you.

WIT. Thou dost bite, my dear mustard-seed; kiss me for that.

PET. Stand off—I'll kiss no more males—I have kissed your Twin yonder in a humour of reconciliation till he [hiccup] rises upon my stomach like a radish.

MILLA. Eh! filthy creature; what was the quarrel?

PET. There was no quarrel; there might have been a quarrel.

WIT. If there had been words enow between 'em to have expressed provocation, they had gone together by the ears like a pair of castanets.

PET. You were the quarrel.

MILLA. Me?

PET. If I have a humour to quarrel, I can make less matters conclude premises. If you are not handsome, what then? If I have a humour to prove it? If I shall have my reward, say so; if not, fight for your face the next time yourself—I'll go sleep.

WIT. Do, wrap thyself up like a woodlouse, and dream revenge. And, hear me, if thou canst learn to write by to-morrow morning, pen me a challenge. I'll carry it for thee.

PET. Carry your mistress's monkey a spider; go flea dogs and read romances. I'll go to bed to my maid.

MRS. FAIN. He's horridly drunk—how came you all in this pickle?

WIT. A plot, a plot, to get rid of the knight—your husband's advice; but he sneaked off.

SCENE X.

Sir Wilfull, drunk, Lady Wishfort, Witwoud, Mrs. Millamant, Mrs. Fainall.

LADY. Out upon't, out upon't, at years of discretion, and comport yourself at this rantipole rate!

SIR WIL. No offence, aunt.

LADY. Offence? As I'm a person, I'm ashamed of you. Fogh! How you stink of wine! D'ye think my niece will ever endure such a Borachio? You're an absolute Borachio.

SIR WIL. Borachio?

LADY. At a time when you should commence an amour, and put your best foot foremost—

SIR WIL. 'Sheart, an you grutch me your liquor, make a bill.—Give me more drink, and take my purse. [Sings]:—

Prithee fill me the glass,
Till it laugh in my face,
With ale that is potent and mellow;
He that whines for a lass
Is an ignorant ass,
For a bumper has not its fellow.

But if you would have me marry my cousin, say the word, and I'll do't. Wilfull will do't, that's the word. Wilfull will do't, that's my crest,—my motto I have forgot.

LADY. My nephew's a little overtaken, cousin, but 'tis drinking your health. O' my word, you are obliged to him—

SIR WIL. In vino veritas, aunt. If I drunk your health to-day, cousin,—I am a Borachio.—But if you have a mind to be married, say the word and send for the piper; Wilfull will do't. If not, dust it away, and let's have t'other round. Tony—ods-heart, where's Tony?—Tony's an honest fellow, but he spits after a bumper, and that's a fault.

We'll drink and we'll never ha' done, boys,
Put the glass then around with the sun, boys,
Let Apollo's example invite us;
For he's drunk every night,
And that makes him so bright,
That he's able next morning to light us.

The sun's a good pimple, an honest soaker, he has a cellar at your antipodes. If I travel, aunt, I touch at your antipodes—your antipodes are a good rascally sort of topsy-turvy fellows. If I had a bumper I'd stand upon my head and drink a health to 'em. A match or no match, cousin with the hard name; aunt, Wilfull will do't. If she has her maidenhead let her look to 't; if she has not, let her keep her own counsel in the meantime, and cry out at the nine months' end.

MILLA. Your pardon, madam, I can stay no longer. Sir Wilfull grows very powerful. Egh! how he smells! I shall be overcome if I stay. Come, cousin.

SCENE XI.

Lady Wishfort, Sir Wilfull Witwoud, Mr. Witwoud, Foible.

LADY. Smells? He would poison a tallow-chandler and his family. Beastly creature, I know not what to do with him. Travel, quotha; ay, travel, travel, get thee gone, get thee but far enough, to the Saracens, or the Tartars, or the Turks—for thou art not fit to live in a Christian commonwealth, thou beastly pagan.

SIR WIL. Turks? No; no Turks, aunt. Your Turks are infidels, and believe not in the grape. Your Mahometan, your Mussulman is a dry stinkard. No offence, aunt. My map says that your Turk is not so honest a man as your Christian—I cannot find by the map that your Mufti is orthodox, whereby it is a plain case that orthodox is a hard word, aunt, and [hiccup] Greek for claret. [Sings]:—

To drink is a Christian diversion,

Unknown to the Turk or the Persian.

Let Mahometan fools

Live by heathenish rules,

And be damned over tea-cups and coffee.

But let British lads sing,

Crown a health to the King,

And a fig for your Sultan and Sophy.

Ah, Tony! [Foible whispers Lady W.]

LADY. Sir Rowland impatient? Good lack! what shall I do with this beastly tumbril? Go lie down and sleep, you sot, or as I'm a person, I'll have you bastinadoed with broomsticks. Call up the wenches with broomsticks.

SIR WIL. Ahey! Wenches? Where are the wenches?

LADY. Dear Cousin Witwoud, get him away, and you will bind me to you inviolably. I have an affair of moment that invades me with some precipitation.—You will oblige me to all futurity.

WIT. Come, knight. Pox on him, I don't know what to say to him. Will you go to a cock-match?

SIR WIL. With a wench, Tony? Is she a shake-bag, sirrah? Let me bite your cheek for that.

WIT. Horrible! He has a breath like a bagpipe. Ay, ay; come, will you march, my Salopian?

SIR WIL. Lead on, little Tony. I'll follow thee, my Anthony, my Tantony. Sirrah, thou shalt be my Tantony, and I'll be thy pig.

And a fig for your Sultan and Sophy.

LADY. This will never do. It will never make a match,—at least before he has been abroad.

SCENE XII.

Lady Wishfort, Waitwell disguised as for Sir Rowland.

LADY. Dear Sir Rowland, I am confounded with confusion at the retrospection of my own rudeness,—I have more pardons to ask than the pope distributes in the year of jubilee. But I hope where there is likely to be so near an alliance, we may unbend the severity of decorum, and dispense with a little ceremony.

WAIT. My impatience, madam, is the effect of my transport; and till I have the possession of your adorable person, I am tantalised on the rack, and do but hang, madam, on the tenter of expectation.

LADY. You have excess of gallantry, Sir Rowland, and press things to a conclusion with a most prevailing vehemence. But a day or two for decency of marriage—

WAIT. For decency of funeral, madam! The delay will break my heart—or if that should fail, I shall be poisoned. My nephew will get an inkling of my designs and poison me—and I would willingly starve him before I die—I would gladly go out of the world with that satisfaction. That would be some comfort to me, if I could but live so long as to be revenged on that unnatural viper.

LADY. Is he so unnatural, say you? Truly I would contribute much both to the saving of your life and the accomplishment of your revenge.

Not that I respect myself; though he has been a perfidious wretch to me.

WAIT. Perfidious to you?

LADY. O Sir Rowland, the hours that he has died away at my feet, the tears that he has shed, the oaths that he has sworn, the palpitations that he has felt, the trances and the tremblings, the ardours and the ecstasies, the kneelings and the risings, the heart-heavings and the hand-gripings, the pangs and the pathetic regards of his protesting eyes!—Oh, no memory can register.

WAIT. What, my rival? Is the rebel my rival? A dies.

LADY. No, don't kill him at once, Sir Rowland: starve him gradually, inch by inch.

WAIT. I'll do't. In three weeks he shall be barefoot; in a month out at knees with begging an alms; he shall starve upward and upward, 'till he has nothing living but his head, and then go out in a stink like a candle's end upon a save-all.

LADY. Well, Sir Rowland, you have the way,—you are no novice in the labyrinth of love,—you have the clue. But as I am a person, Sir Rowland, you must not attribute my yielding to any sinister appetite or indigestion of widowhood; nor impute my complacency to any lethargy of continence. I hope you do not think me prone to any iteration of nuptials?

WAIT. Far be it from me—

LADY. If you do, I protest I must recede, or think that I have made a prostitution of decorums, but in the vehemence of compassion, and to save the life of a person of so much importance—

WAIT. I esteem it so—

LADY. Or else you wrong my condescension—

WAIT. I do not, I do not—

LADY. Indeed you do.

WAIT. I do not, fair shrine of virtue.

LADY. If you think the least scruple of causality was an ingredient—

WAIT. Dear madam, no. You are all camphire and frankincense, all chastity and odour.

LADY. Or that—

SCENE XIII.

[To them] Foible.

FOIB. Madam, the dancers are ready, and there's one with a letter, who must deliver it into your own hands.

LADY. Sir Rowland, will you give me leave? Think favourably, judge candidly, and conclude you have found a person who would suffer racks in honour's cause, dear Sir Rowland, and will wait on you incessantly.

SCENE XIV.

Waitwell, Foible.

WAIT. Fie, fie! What a slavery have I undergone; spouse, hast thou any cordial? I want spirits.

FOIB. What a washy rogue art thou, to pant thus for a quarter of an hour's lying and swearing to a fine lady?

WAIT. Oh, she is the antidote to desire. Spouse, thou wilt fare the worse for't. I shall have no appetite to iteration of nuptials—this eight-and-forty hours. By this hand I'd rather be a chairman in the dog-days than act Sir Rowland till this time to-morrow.

SCENE XV.

[To them] Lady with a letter.

LADY. Call in the dancers; Sir Rowland, we'll sit, if you please, and see the entertainment. [Dance.] Now, with your permission, Sir Rowland, I will peruse my letter. I would open it in your presence, because I would not make you uneasy. If it should make you uneasy, I would burn it—speak if it does—but you may see, the superscription is like a woman's hand.

FOIB. By heaven! Mrs. Marwood's, I know it,—my heart aches—get it from her! [To him.]

WAIT. A woman's hand? No madam, that's no woman's hand: I see that already. That's somebody whose throat must be cut.

LADY. Nay, Sir Rowland, since you give me a proof of your passion by your jealousy, I promise you I'll make a return by a frank communication. You shall see it—we'll open it together. Look you here. [Reads.] Madam, though unknown to you (look you there, 'tis from nobody that I know.) I have that honour for your character, that I think myself obliged to let you know you are abused. He who pretends to be Sir Rowland is a cheat and a rascal. O heavens! what's this?

FOIB. Unfortunate; all's ruined.

WAIT. How, how, let me see, let me see. [Reading.] A rascal, and disguised and suborned for that imposture—O villainy! O villainy!—by the contrivance of—

LADY. I shall faint, I shall die. Oh!

FOIB. Say 'tis your nephew's hand. Quickly, his plot, swear, swear it! [To him.]

WAIT. Here's a villain! Madam, don't you perceive it? Don't you see it?

LADY. Too well, too well. I have seen too much.

WAIT. I told you at first I knew the hand. A woman's hand? The rascal writes a sort of a large hand: your Roman hand.—I saw there was a throat to be cut presently. If he were my son, as he is my nephew, I'd pistol him.

FOIB. O treachery! But are you sure, Sir Rowland, it is his writing?

WAIT. Sure? Am I here? Do I live? Do I love this pearl of India? I have twenty letters in my pocket from him in the same character.

LADY. How?

FOIB. Oh, what luck it is, Sir Rowland, that you were present at this juncture! This was the business that brought Mr. Mirabell disguised to Madam Millamant this afternoon. I thought something was contriving, when he stole by me and would have hid his face.

LADY. How, how? I heard the villain was in the house indeed; and now I remember, my niece went away abruptly when Sir Wilfull was to have made his addresses.

FOIB. Then, then, madam, Mr. Mirabell waited for her in her chamber; but I would not tell your ladyship to discompose you when you were to receive Sir Rowland.

WAIT. Enough, his date is short.

FOIB. No, good Sir Rowland, don't incur the law.

WAIT. Law? I care not for law. I can but die, and 'tis in a good cause. My lady shall be satisfied of my truth and innocence, though it cost me my life.

LADY. No, dear Sir Rowland, don't fight: if you should be killed I must never show my face; or hanged,—oh, consider my reputation, Sir Rowland. No, you shan't fight: I'll go in and examine my niece; I'll make her confess. I conjure you, Sir Rowland, by all your love not to fight.

WAIT. I am charmed, madam; I obey. But some proof you must let me give you: I'll go for a black box, which contains the writings of my whole estate, and deliver that into your hands.

LADY. Ay, dear Sir Rowland, that will be some comfort; bring the black box.

WAIT. And may I presume to bring a contract to be signed this night? May I hope so far?

LADY. Bring what you will; but come alive, pray come alive. Oh, this is a happy discovery.

WAIT. Dead or alive I'll come—and married we will be in spite of treachery; ay, and get an heir that shall defeat the last remaining glimpse of hope in my abandoned nephew. Come, my buxom widow:

E'er long you shall substantial proof receive

That I'm an arrant knight—

FOIB. Or arrant knave.

ACT V.—SCENE I.

Scene Continues.

Lady Wishfort and Foible.

LADY. Out of my house, out of my house, thou viper, thou serpent that I have fostered, thou bosom traitress that I raised from nothing! Begone, begone, begone, go, go; that I took from washing of old gauze and weaving of dead hair, with a bleak blue nose, over a chafing-dish of starved embers, and dining behind a traver's rag, in a shop no bigger than a bird-cage. Go, go, starve again, do, do!

FOIB. Dear madam, I'll beg pardon on my knees.

LADY. Away, out, out, go set up for yourself again, do; drive a trade, do, with your threepennyworth of small ware, flaunting upon a packthread, under a brandy-seller's bulk, or against a dead wall by a balladmonger. Go, hang out an old frisoneer-gorget, with a yard of yellow colberteen again, do; an old gnawed mask, two rows of pins, and a child's fiddle; a glass necklace with the beads broken, and a quilted night-cap with one ear. Go, go, drive a trade. These were your commodities, you treacherous trull; this was the merchandise you dealt in, when I took you into my house, placed you next myself, and made you governant of my whole family. You have forgot this, have you, now you have feathered your nest?

FOIB. No, no, dear madam. Do but hear me, have but a moment's patience—I'll confess all. Mr. Mirabell seduced me; I am not the first that he has wheedled with his dissembling tongue. Your ladyship's own wisdom has been deluded by him; then how should I, a poor ignorant, defend myself? O madam, if you knew but what he promised me, and how he assured me your ladyship should come to no damage, or else the wealth of the Indies should not have bribed me to conspire against so good, so sweet, so kind a lady as you have been to me.

LADY. No damage? What, to betray me, to marry me to a cast serving-man; to make me a receptacle, an hospital for a decayed pimp?

No damage? O thou frontless impudence, more than a big-bellied actress!

FOIB. Pray do but hear me, madam; he could not marry your ladyship, madam. No indeed, his marriage was to have been void in law; for he was married to me first, to secure your ladyship. He could not have bedded your ladyship, for if he had consummated with your ladyship, he must have run the risk of the law, and been put upon his clergy. Yes indeed, I enquired of the law in that case before I would meddle or make.

LADY. What? Then I have been your property, have I? I have been convenient to you, it seems, while you were catering for Mirabell; I have been broker for you? What, have you made a passive bawd of me? This exceeds all precedent. I am brought to fine uses, to become a botcher of second-hand marriages between Abigails and Andrews! I'll couple you. Yes, I'll baste you together, you and your Philander. I'll Duke's Place you, as I'm a person. Your turtle is in custody already. You shall coo in the same cage, if there be constable or warrant in the parish.

FOIB. Oh, that ever I was born! Oh, that I was ever married! A bride? Ay, I shall be a Bridewell bride. Oh!

SCENE II.

Mrs. Fainall, Foible.

MRS. FAIN. Poor Foible, what's the matter?

FOIB. O madam, my lady's gone for a constable; I shall be had to a justice, and put to Bridewell to beat hemp. Poor Waitwell's gone to prison already.

MRS. FAIN. Have a good heart, Foible: Mirabell's gone to give security for him. This is all Marwood's and my husband's doing.

FOIB. Yes, yes; I know it, madam: she was in my lady's closet, and overheard all that you said to me before dinner. She sent the letter to my lady, and that missing effect, Mr. Fainall laid this plot to arrest Waitwell, when he pretended to go for the papers; and in the meantime Mrs. Marwood declared all to my lady.

MRS. FAIN. Was there no mention made of me in the letter? My mother does not suspect my being in the confederacy? I fancy

Marwood has not told her, though she has told my husband.

FOIB. Yes, madam; but my lady did not see that part. We stifled the letter before she read so far. Has that mischievous devil told Mr. Fainall of your ladyship then?

MRS. FAIN. Ay, all's out: my affair with Mirabell, everything discovered. This is the last day of our living together; that's my comfort.

FOIB. Indeed, madam, and so 'tis a comfort, if you knew all. He has been even with your ladyship; which I could have told you long enough since, but I love to keep peace and quietness by my good will. I had rather bring friends together than set 'em at distance. But Mrs. Marwood and he are nearer related than ever their parents thought for.

MRS. FAIN. Say'st thou so, Foible? Canst thou prove this?

FOIB. I can take my oath of it, madam; so can Mrs. Mincing. We have had many a fair word from Madam Marwood to conceal something that passed in our chamber one evening when you were at Hyde Park, and we were thought to have gone a-walking. But we went up unawares—though we were sworn to secrecy too: Madam Marwood took a book and swore us upon it: but it was but a book of poems. So long as it was not a bible oath, we may break it with a safe conscience.

MRS. FAIN. This discovery is the most opportune thing I could wish. Now, Mincing?

SCENE III.

[To them] Mincing.

MINC. My lady would speak with Mrs. Foible, mem. Mr. Mirabell is with her; he has set your spouse at liberty, Mrs. Foible, and would have you hide yourself in my lady's closet till my old lady's anger is abated. Oh, my old lady is in a perilous passion at something Mr. Fainall has said; he swears, and my old lady cries. There's a fearful hurricane, I vow. He says, mem, how that he'll have my lady's fortune made over to him, or he'll be divorced.

MRS. FAIN. Does your lady or Mirabell know that?

MINC. Yes mem; they have sent me to see if Sir Wilfull be sober, and to bring him to them. My lady is resolved to have him, I think, rather than lose such a vast sum as six thousand pound. Oh, come, Mrs. Foible, I hear my old lady.

MRS. FAIN. Foible, you must tell Mincing that she must prepare to vouch when I call her.

FOIB. Yes, yes, madam.

MINC. Oh, yes mem, I'll vouch anything for your ladyship's service, be what it will.

SCENE IV.

Mrs. Fainall, Lady Wishfort, Mrs. Marwood.

LADY. O my dear friend, how can I enumerate the benefits that I have received from your goodness? To you I owe the timely discovery of the false vows of Mirabell; to you I owe the detection of the impostor Sir Rowland. And now you are become an intercessor with my son-in-law, to save the honour of my house and compound for the frailties of my daughter. Well, friend, you are enough to reconcile me to the bad world, or else I would retire to deserts and solitudes, and feed harmless sheep by groves and purling streams. Dear Marwood, let us leave the world, and retire by ourselves and be shepherdesses.

MRS. MAR. Let us first dispatch the affair in hand, madam. We shall have leisure to think of retirement afterwards. Here is one who is concerned in the treaty.

LADY. O daughter, daughter, is it possible thou shouldst be my child, bone of my bone, and flesh of my flesh, and as I may say, another me, and yet transgress the most minute particle of severe virtue? Is it possible you should lean aside to iniquity, who have been cast in the direct mould of virtue? I have not only been a mould but a pattern for you, and a model for you, after you were brought into the world.

MRS. FAIN. I don't understand your ladyship.

LADY. Not understand? Why, have you not been naught? Have you not been sophisticated? Not understand? Here I am ruined to compound for your caprices and your cuckoldoms. I must pawn my plate and my jewels, and ruin my niece, and all little enough—

MRS. FAIN. I am wronged and abused, and so are you. 'Tis a false accusation, as false as hell, as false as your friend there; ay, or your friend's friend, my false husband.

MRS. MAR. My friend, Mrs. Fainall? Your husband my friend, what do you mean?

MRS. FAIN. I know what I mean, madam, and so do you; and so shall the world at a time convenient.

MRS. MAR. I am sorry to see you so passionate, madam. More temper would look more like innocence. But I have done. I am sorry my zeal to serve your ladyship and family should admit of misconstruction, or make me liable to affronts. You will pardon me, madam, if I meddle no more with an affair in which I am not personally concerned.

LADY. O dear friend, I am so ashamed that you should meet with such returns. You ought to ask pardon on your knees, ungrateful creature; she deserves more from you than all your life can accomplish. Oh, don't leave me destitute in this perplexity! No, stick to me, my good genius.

MRS. FAIN. I tell you, madam, you're abused. Stick to you? Ay, like a leech, to suck your best blood; she'll drop off when she's full. Madam, you shan't pawn a bodkin, nor part with a brass counter, in composition for me. I defy 'em all. Let 'em prove their aspersions: I know my own innocence, and dare stand a trial.

SCENE V.

Lady Wishfort, Mrs. Marwood.

LADY. Why, if she should be innocent, if she should be wronged after all, ha? I don't know what to think, and I promise you, her education has been unexceptionable. I may say it, for I chiefly made it my own care to initiate her very infancy in the rudiments of virtue, and to impress upon her tender years a young odium and aversion to the very sight of men; ay, friend, she would ha' shrieked if she had but seen a man till she was in her teens. As I'm a person, 'tis true. She was never suffered to play with a male child, though but in coats. Nay, her very babies were of the feminine gender. Oh, she never looked a man in the face but her own father or the chaplain, and him we made a shift to put upon her for a woman, by the help of his long garments, and his sleek face, till she was going in her fifteen.

MRS. MAR. 'Twas much she should be deceived so long.

LADY. I warrant you, or she would never have borne to have been catechised by him, and have heard his long lectures against singing and dancing and such debaucheries, and going to filthy plays, and profane music meetings, where the lewd trebles squeak nothing but bawdy, and the basses roar blasphemy. Oh, she would have swooned at the sight or name of an obscene play-book—and can I think after all this that my daughter can be naught? What, a whore? And thought it excommunication to set her foot within the door of a playhouse. O dear friend, I can't believe it. No, no; as she says, let him prove it, let him prove it.

MRS. MAR. Prove it, madam? What, and have your name prostituted in a public court; yours and your daughter's reputation worried at the bar by a pack of bawling lawyers? To be ushered in with an Oh yes of scandal, and have your case opened by an old fumbling leacher in a quoif like a man midwife; to bring your daughter's infamy to light; to be a theme for legal punsters and quibblers by the statute; and become a jest, against a rule of court, where there is no precedent for a jest in any record, not even in Doomsday Book. To discompose the gravity of the bench, and provoke naughty interrogatories in more naughty law Latin; while the good judge, tickled with the proceeding, simpers under a grey beard, and fidges off and on his cushion as if he had swallowed cantharides, or sate upon cow-itch.

LADY. Oh, 'tis very hard!

MRS. MAR. And then to have my young revellers of the Temple take notes, like prentices at a conventicle; and after talk it over again in Commons, or before drawers in an eating-house.

LADY. Worse and worse.

MRS. MAR. Nay, this is nothing; if it would end here 'twere well. But it must after this be consigned by the shorthand writers to the public press; and from thence be transferred to the hands, nay, into the throats and lungs, of hawkers, with voices more licentious than the loud flounder-man's. And this you must hear till you are stunned; nay, you must hear nothing else for some days.

LADY. Oh 'tis insupportable. No, no, dear friend, make it up, make it up; ay, ay, I'll compound. I'll give up all, myself and my all, my niece and her all, anything, everything, for composition.

MRS. MAR. Nay, madam, I advise nothing, I only lay before you, as a friend, the inconveniences which perhaps you have overseen. Here comes Mr. Fainall; if he will be satisfied to huddle up all in silence, I shall be glad. You must think I would rather congratulate than condole with you.

SCENE VI.

Fainall, Lady Wishfort, Mrs. Marwood.

LADY. Ay, ay, I do not doubt it, dear Marwood. No, no, I do not doubt it.

FAIN. Well, madam, I have suffered myself to be overcome by the importunity of this lady, your friend, and am content you shall enjoy your own proper estate during life, on condition you oblige yourself never to marry, under such penalty as I think convenient.

LADY. Never to marry?

FAIN. No more Sir Rowlands,—the next imposture may not be so timely detected.

MRS. MAR. That condition, I dare answer, my lady will consent to, without difficulty; she has already but too much experienced the perfidiousness of men. Besides, madam, when we retire to our pastoral solitude, we shall bid adieu to all other thoughts.

LADY. Ay, that's true; but in case of necessity, as of health, or some such emergency—

FAIN. Oh, if you are prescribed marriage, you shall be considered; I will only reserve to myself the power to choose for you. If your physic be wholesome, it matters not who is your apothecary. Next, my wife shall settle on me the remainder of her fortune, not made over already; and for her maintenance depend entirely on my discretion.

LADY. This is most inhumanly savage: exceeding the barbarity of a Muscovite husband.

FAIN. I learned it from his Czarish Majesty's retinue, in a winter evening's conference over brandy and pepper, amongst other secrets of matrimony and policy, as they are at present practised in the northern hemisphere. But this must be agreed unto, and that positively. Lastly, I will be endowed, in right of my wife, with that six thousand pound, which is the moiety of Mrs. Millamant's fortune in your possession, and which she has forfeited (as will appear by the last will and testament of your deceased husband, Sir Jonathan Wishfort) by her disobedience in contracting herself against your consent or knowledge, and by refusing the offered match with Sir Wilfull Witwoud, which you, like a careful aunt, had provided for her.

LADY. My nephew was non compos, and could not make his addresses.

FAIN. I come to make demands—I'll hear no objections.

LADY. You will grant me time to consider?

FAIN. Yes, while the instrument is drawing, to which you must set your hand till more sufficient deeds can be perfected: which I will take care shall be done with all possible speed. In the meanwhile I will go for the said instrument, and till my return you may balance this matter in your own discretion.

SCENE VII.

Lady Wishfort, Mrs. Marwood.

LADY. This insolence is beyond all precedent, all parallel. Must I be subject to this merciless villain?

MRS. MAR. 'Tis severe indeed, madam, that you should smart for your daughter's wantonness.

LADY. 'Twas against my consent that she married this barbarian, but she would have him, though her year was not out. Ah! her first husband, my son Languish, would not have carried it thus. Well, that was my choice, this is hers; she is matched now with a witness—I shall be mad, dear friend; is there no comfort for me? Must I live to be confiscated at this rebel-rate? Here come two more of my Egyptian plagues too.

SCENE VIII.

[To them] Mrs. Millamant, Sir Wilfull.

SIR WIL. Aunt, your servant.

LADY. Out, caterpillar, call not me aunt; I know thee not.

SIR WIL. I confess I have been a little in disguise, as they say. 'Sheart! and I'm sorry for't. What would you have? I hope I committed no offence, aunt—and if I did I am willing to make satisfaction; and what can a man say fairer? If I have broke anything I'll pay for't, an it cost a pound. And so let that content for what's past, and make no more words. For what's to come, to pleasure you I'm willing to marry my cousin. So, pray, let's all be friends, she and I are agreed upon the matter before a witness.

LADY. How's this, dear niece? Have I any comfort? Can this be true?

MILLA. I am content to be a sacrifice to your repose, madam, and to convince you that I had no hand in the plot, as you were misinformed. I have laid my commands on Mirabell to come in person, and be a witness that I give my hand to this flower of knighthood; and for the contract that passed between Mirabell and me, I have obliged him to make a resignation of it in your ladyship's presence. He is without and waits your leave for admittance.

LADY. Well, I'll swear I am something revived at this testimony of your obedience; but I cannot admit that traitor,—I fear I cannot fortify myself to support his appearance. He is as terrible to me as a Gorgon: if I see him I swear I shall turn to stone, petrify incessantly.

MILLA. If you disoblige him he may resent your refusal, and insist upon the contract still. Then 'tis the last time he will be offensive to you.

LADY. Are you sure it will be the last time? If I were sure of that—shall I never see him again?

MILLA. Sir Wilfull, you and he are to travel together, are you not?

SIR WIL. 'Sheart, the gentleman's a civil gentleman, aunt, let him come in; why, we are sworn brothers and fellow-travellers. We are to be Pylades and Orestes, he and I. He is to be my interpreter in foreign parts. He has been overseas once already; and with proviso that I marry my cousin, will cross 'em once again, only to bear me company. 'Sheart, I'll call him in,—an I set on't once, he shall come in; and see who'll hinder him. [Goes to the door and hems.]

MRS. MAR. This is precious fooling, if it would pass; but I'll know the bottom of it.

LADY. O dear Marwood, you are not going?

MRS. MAR. Not far, madam; I'll return immediately.

SCENE IX.

Lady Wishfort, Mrs. Millamant, Sir Wilfull, Mirabell.

SIR WIL. Look up, man, I'll stand by you; 'sbud, an she do frown, she can't kill you. Besides—harkee, she dare not frown desperately, because her face is none of her own. 'Sheart, an she should, her forehead would wrinkle like the coat of a cream cheese; but mum for that, fellow-traveller.

MIRA. If a deep sense of the many injuries I have offered to so good a lady, with a sincere remorse and a hearty contrition, can but obtain the least glance of compassion. I am too happy. Ah, madam, there was a time—but let it be forgotten. I confess I have deservedly forfeited the high place I once held, of sighing at your feet; nay, kill me not by turning from me in disdain, I come not to plead for favour. Nay, not for pardon: I am a suppliant only for pity:—I am going where I never shall behold you more.

SIR WIL. How, fellow-traveller? You shall go by yourself then.

MIRA. Let me be pitied first, and afterwards forgotten. I ask no more.

SIR WIL. By'r lady, a very reasonable request, and will cost you nothing, aunt. Come, come, forgive and forget, aunt. Why you must an you are a Christian.

MIRA. Consider, madam; in reality you could not receive much prejudice: it was an innocent device, though I confess it had a face of guiltiness—it was at most an artifice which love contrived—and errors which love produces have ever been accounted venial. At least think it is punishment enough that I have lost what in my heart I hold most dear, that to your cruel indignation I have offered up this beauty, and with her my peace and quiet; nay, all my hopes of future comfort.

SIR WIL. An he does not move me, would I may never be o' the quorum. An it were not as good a deed as to drink, to give her to him again, I would I might never take shipping. Aunt, if you don't forgive quickly, I shall melt, I can tell you that. My contract went no farther than a little mouth-glue, and that's hardly dry; one doleful sigh more from my fellow-traveller and 'tis dissolved.

LADY. Well, nephew, upon your account. Ah, he has a false insinuating tongue. Well, sir, I will stifle my just resentment at my nephew's request. I will endeavour what I can to forget, but on proviso that you resign the contract with my niece immediately.

MIRA. It is in writing and with papers of concern; but I have sent my servant for it, and will deliver it to you, with all acknowledgments for your transcendent goodness.

LADY. Oh, he has witchcraft in his eyes and tongue; when I did not see him I could have bribed a villain to his assassination; but his appearance rakes the embers which have so long lain smothered in my breast. [Aside.]

SCENE X.

[To them] Fainall, Mrs. Marwood.

FAIN. Your date of deliberation, madam, is expired. Here is the instrument; are you prepared to sign?

LADY. If I were prepared, I am not impowered. My niece exerts a lawful claim, having matched herself by my direction to Sir Wilfull.

FAIN. That sham is too gross to pass on me, though 'tis imposed on you, madam.

MILLA. Sir, I have given my consent.

MIRA. And, sir, I have resigned my pretensions.

SIR WIL. And, sir, I assert my right; and will maintain it in defiance of you, sir, and of your instrument. 'Sheart, an you talk of an instrument sir, I have an old fox by my thigh shall hack your instrument of ram vellum to shreds, sir. It shall not be sufficient for a Mittimus or a tailor's measure; therefore withdraw your instrument, sir, or, by'r lady, I shall draw mine.

LADY. Hold, nephew, hold.

MILLA. Good Sir Wilfull, respite your valour.

FAIN. Indeed? Are you provided of your guard, with your single beef-eater there? But I'm prepared for you, and insist upon my first proposal. You shall submit your own estate to my management, and absolutely make over my wife's to my sole use, as pursuant to the purport and tenor of this other covenant. I suppose, madam, your consent is not requisite in this case; nor, Mr. Mirabell, your resignation; nor, Sir Wilfull, your right. You may draw your fox if you please, sir, and make a bear-garden flourish somewhere else; for here it will not avail. This, my Lady Wishfort, must be subscribed, or your darling daughter's turned adrift, like a leaky hulk to sink or swim, as she and the current of this lewd town can agree.

LADY. Is there no means, no remedy, to stop my ruin? Ungrateful wretch! Dost thou not owe thy being, thy subsistance, to my daughter's fortune?

FAIN. I'll answer you when I have the rest of it in my possession.

MIRA. But that you would not accept of a remedy from my hands—I own I have not deserved you should owe any obligation to me; or else, perhaps, I could devise—

LADY. Oh, what? what? To save me and my child from ruin, from want, I'll forgive all that's past; nay, I'll consent to anything to come, to be delivered from this tyranny.

MIRA. Ay, madam; but that is too late, my reward is intercepted. You have disposed of her who only could have made me a compensation for all my services. But be it as it may, I am resolved I'll serve you; you shall not be wronged in this savage manner.

LADY. How? Dear Mr. Mirabell, can you be so generous at last? But it is not possible. Harkee, I'll break my nephew's match; you shall have my niece yet, and all her fortune, if you can but save me from this imminent danger.

MIRA. Will you? I take you at your word. I ask no more. I must have leave for two criminals to appear.

LADY. Ay, ay, anybody, anybody.

MIRA. Foible is one, and a penitent.

SCENE XI.

[To them] Mrs. Fainall, Foible, Mincing.

MRS. MAR. O my shame! [Mirabell and Lady go to Mrs. Fainall and Foible.] These currupt things are brought hither to expose me. [To Fainall.]

FAIN. If it must all come out, why let 'em know it, 'tis but the way of the world. That shall not urge me to relinquish or abate one tittle of my terms; no, I will insist the more.

FOIB. Yes, indeed, madam; I'll take my bible-oath of it.

MINC. And so will I, mem.

LADY. O Marwood, Marwood, art thou false? My friend deceive me? Hast thou been a wicked accomplice with that profligate man?

MRS. MAR. Have you so much ingratitude and injustice to give credit, against your friend, to the aspersions of two such mercenary trulls?

MINC. Mercenary, mem? I scorn your words. 'Tis true we found you and Mr. Fainall in the blue garret; by the same token, you swore us to secrecy upon Messalinas's poems. Mercenary? No, if we would have been mercenary, we should have held our tongues; you would have bribed us sufficiently.

FAIN. Go, you are an insignificant thing. Well, what are you the better for this? Is this Mr. Mirabell's expedient? I'll be put off no longer. You, thing, that was a wife, shall smart for this. I will not leave thee wherewithal to hide thy shame: your body shall be naked as your reputation.

MRS. FAIN. I despise you and defy your malice. You have aspersed me wrongfully—I have proved your falsehood. Go, you and your treacherous—I will not name it, but starve together. Perish.

FAIN. Not while you are worth a groat, indeed, my dear. Madam, I'll be fooled no longer.

LADY. Ah, Mr. Mirabell, this is small comfort, the detection of this affair.

MIRA. Oh, in good time. Your leave for the other offender and penitent to appear, madam.

SCENE XII.

[To them] Mrs. Fainall, Foible, Mincing.

LADY. O Sir Rowland! Well, rascal?

WAIT. What your ladyship pleases. I have brought the black box at last, madam.

MIRA. Give it me. Madam, you remember your promise.

LADY. Ay, dear sir.

MIRA. Where are the gentlemen?

WAIT. At hand, sir, rubbing their eyes,—just risen from sleep.

FAIN. 'Sdeath, what's this to me? I'll not wait your private concerns.

SCENE XIII.

[To them] Petulant, Witwoud.

PET. How now? What's the matter? Whose hand's out?

WIT. Hey day! What, are you all got together, like players at the end of the last act?

MIRA. You may remember, gentlemen, I once requested your hands as witnesses to a certain parchment.

WIT. Ay, I do, my hand I remember—Petulant set his mark.

MIRA. You wrong him; his name is fairly written, as shall appear. You do not remember, gentlemen, anything of what that parchment contained? [Undoing the box.]

WIT. No.

PET. Not I. I writ; I read nothing.

MIRA. Very well, now you shall know. Madam, your promise.

LADY. Ay, ay, sir, upon my honour.

MIRA. Mr. Fainall, it is now time that you should know that your lady, while she was at her own disposal, and before you had by your insinuations wheedled her out of a pretended settlement of the greatest part of her fortune—

FAIN. Sir! Pretended?

MIRA. Yes, sir. I say that this lady, while a widow, having, it seems, received some cautions respecting your inconstancy and tyranny of temper, which from her own partial opinion and fondness of you she could never have suspected—she did, I say, by the wholesome advice of friends and of sages learned in the laws of this land, deliver this same as her act and deed to me in trust, and to the uses within mentioned. You may read if you please [holding out the parchment], though perhaps what is written on the back may serve your occasions.

FAIN. Very likely, sir. What's here? Damnation! [Reads] A Deed of Conveyance of the whole estate real of Arabella Languish, widow, in trust to Edward Mirabell. Confusion!

MIRA. Even so, sir: 'tis the way of the world, sir; of the widows of the world. I suppose this deed may bear an elder date than what you have obtained from your lady.

FAIN. Perfidious fiend! Then thus I'll be revenged. [Offers to run at Mrs. Fainall.]

SIR WIL. Hold, sir; now you may make your bear-garden flourish somewhere else, sir.

FAIN. Mirabell, you shall hear of this, sir; be sure you shall. Let me pass, oaf.

MRS. FAIN. Madam, you seem to stifle your resentment. You had better give it vent.

MRS. MAR. Yes, it shall have vent, and to your confusion, or I'll perish in the attempt.

SCENE the Last.

Lady Wishfort, Mrs. Millamant, Mirabell, Mrs. Fainall, Sir Wilfull, Petulant, Witwoud, Foible, Mincing, Waitwell.

LADY. O daughter, daughter, 'tis plain thou hast inherited thy mother's prudence.

MRS. FAIN. Thank Mr. Mirabell, a cautious friend, to whose advice all is owing.

LADY. Well, Mr. Mirabell, you have kept your promise, and I must perform mine. First, I pardon for your sake Sir Rowland there and Foible. The next thing is to break the matter to my nephew, and how to do that—

MIRA. For that, madam, give yourself no trouble; let me have your consent. Sir Wilfull is my friend: he has had compassion upon lovers, and generously engaged a volunteer in this action, for our service, and now designs to prosecute his travels.

SIR WIL. 'Sheart, aunt, I have no mind to marry. My cousin's a fine lady, and the gentleman loves her and she loves him, and they deserve one another; my resolution is to see foreign parts. I have set on't, and when I'm set on't I must do't. And if these two gentlemen would travel too, I think they may be spared.

PET. For my part, I say little. I think things are best off or on.

WIT. I'gad, I understand nothing of the matter: I'm in a maze yet, like a dog in a dancing school.

LADY. Well, sir, take her, and with her all the joy I can give you.

MILLA. Why does not the man take me? Would you have me give myself to you over again?

MIRA. Ay, and over and over again. [Kisses her hand.] I would have you as often as possibly I can. Well, heav'n grant I love you not too well; that's all my fear.

SIR WIL. 'Sheart, you'll have time enough to toy after you're married, or, if you will toy now, let us have a dance in the meantime; that we who are not lovers may have some other employment besides looking on.

MIRA. With all my heart, dear Sir Wilfull. What shall we do for music?

FOIB. Oh, sir, some that were provided for Sir Rowland's entertainment are yet within call. [A dance.]

LADY. As I am a person, I can hold out no longer: I have wasted my spirits so to-day already that I am ready to sink under the fatigue; and I cannot but have some fears upon me yet, that my son Fainall will pursue some desperate course.

MIRA. Madam, disquiet not yourself on that account: to my knowledge his circumstances are such he must of force comply. For my part I will contribute all that in me lies to a reunion. In the meantime, madam [to Mrs. Fainall], let me before these witnesses restore to you this deed of trust: it may be a means, well managed, to make you live easily together.

From hence let those be warned, who mean to wed,
Lest mutual falsehood stain the bridal-bed:
For each deceiver to his cost may find
That marriage frauds too oft are paid in kind.

[Exeunt Omnes.

EPILOGUE.

Spoken by Mrs. Bracegirdle.

After our Epilogue this crowd dismisses,
I'm thinking how this play'll be pulled to pieces.
But pray consider, e'er you doom its fall,
How hard a thing 'twould be to please you all.
There are some critics so with spleen diseased,
They scarcely come inclining to be pleased:
And sure he must have more than mortal skill
Who pleases anyone against his will.
Then, all bad poets we are sure are foes,
And how their number's swelled the town well knows
In shoals, I've marked 'em judging in the pit;
Though they're on no pretence for judgment fit,
But that they have been damned for want of wit.
Since when, they, by their own offences taught,
Set up for spies on plays, and finding fault.
Others there are whose malice we'd prevent:
Such, who watch plays, with scurrilous intent
To mark out who by characters are meant:
And though no perfect likeness they can trace,
Yet each pretends to know the copied face.
These, with false glosses, feed their own ill-nature,
And turn to libel what was meant a satire.
May such malicious fops this fortune find,

To think themselves alone the fools designed:
If any are so arrogantly vain,
To think they singly can support a scene,
And furnish fool enough to entertain.
For well the learned and the judicious know,
That satire scorns to stoop so meanly low,
As any one abstracted fop to show.
For, as when painters form a matchless face,
They from each fair one catch some diff'rent grace,
And shining features in one portrait blend,
To which no single beauty must pretend:
So poets oft do in one piece expose
Whole belles assemblées of coquettes and beaux.

❐❐❐